THE DEAD OF CHRISTMAS

IT'S A SLAYING GOOD TIME

TORY FAVRO

First edition published 2023

ISBN: 978-0-6486102-0-5

Acknowledgements: Thank you to Allison Olbrich, Jessica Henley, and Julie-Anne Morrison for test reading and offering your suggestions.

For more information please visit
TORYFAVRO.COM

Chapters

The North Pole Bloodbath

"**M**otherfucker!" Nick slammed more shells into the pump action shotgun. The barrel was hot, warming his face through his beard. It had a red glow starting to make its way to the surface of the metal. He could not even count how many rounds had worked their way through it in the last hour. It had been a lot, he knew that much.

He also thought he might be going deaf from all the shells he had shot.

Thank God the exterior perimeter defenses had been active and working even in this blizzard. Nick had been working his butt off to make sure the whole network had been properly connected as he had seen the reports of the crappy weather headed their way. This had been his second year on station, every day he thought it wouldn't get weirder. But here he was with it yet again, getting weirder. Of all things fighting the fucking Undead.

Of course he had stumbled across reports of this craziness going on around the world; after all who hadn't? At first, it had been shrugged off as nothing more than some weird sort of trolling on the Internet, but then as the wave of Undead swarmed around back home, it was impossible to ignore. It was just that his own Agency had told him it was all rumors and kids on the 'net.

Nick was still not sure how it started, but conspiracy theorists were pointing the finger at Europe. In particular, a small country with neighbors on all sides of its borders. Gradually to their horror, it seemed as though something out of a movie had come to life. Once there was no more room in Hell, then the dead walked the Earth.

And the living didn't have a prayer, because it was the Dawn of the Dead. *Thanks a bunch for that Romero*, Nick thought. Fucking Zombies….

But still, out here?

"Carol! Carol!"

Then a pause, "Carol?"

Nick risked a glance over at his wife, who was surrounded by her assistants as the barrel of the front facing minigun was lowered to the ground while they tried to figure out why it was jamming. It was kind of stupid but he was glad the darn thing wasn't firing. THAT gun was really noisy.

Assistants, he laughed to himself. He had actually really struggled using the word Elves initially, but that is what they were. They were short people. No, they weren't. Well yes they were but…. At first Nick thought they were a bunch of little people sent up there by the Agency to help them out, but as time progressed, he realized that they were a race unto themselves with their own language, methods and traditions.

2

For some fucking reason they seemed to like making toys for children. He couldn't figure it out. He hoped that there was nothing more to it than an overwhelming desire to help the children of the world. Though, to be honest, he couldn't really talk. He had felt like a hypocrite when he took the job.

He had met his wife Carol at the Agency, rather through the Agency during an operation which to this day she still was not allowed to talk about. Luckily for Nick this lack of information means another story for another book. But needless to say it was a whirlwind romance filled with bullets, ███ carrots, a small range ███ bomb and a chainsaw. They had ended up in each other's arms, and the rest was history. A heavily redacted fucking history.

In any case, getting back to the little guys; they were feverishly trying to get the minigun working. There were also anti-aircraft defenses there, but as the battle had mainly taken place on the ground, they were next to useless. The Elves were armed to the teeth, and they were ferocious fighters, though in actuality, there had been no reason for bloody conflict on the land of the North Pole for quite some time.

"Yes, dear?" said Carol.

She stopped grazing the barrels, wiping her hands on her apron. The khaki green and red of her uniform hid all but the worst of the grime; he could see the dried blood across her cheeks though and it made him furious. He didn't think it was hers, but at this distance, he couldn't be sure.

"Honey, how far off are we from getting that fucking thing working?"

He shoved the barrel of his gun into the snow at his feet and heard it hiss. It probably wasn't good for the metal, but he couldn't think of any other way to stop this thing from exploding in his own face when he fired it. It was hard to believe that all this had started roughly eight hours ago...

The Blob
(But not the 1958 movie)

T he first attack began innocuously enough. One of the guys on Lookout had spotted a red blob approaching from the far south. Of course being this far up north everything approached from the south. Sometimes people would venture up this far, however it was rare and wearing that bright red outfit, whoever it was stood out like balls on a dog.

The lengths at which people went to explore the unknown constantly amazed Nick and they had posted warning signs up there on the Edge of the World so that people wouldn't fall off in the middle of the night. It amazed him that it had never been done before, and he wondered what it would feel like to simply fall over the edge of the planet into the abyss. He leaned over the edge once with Carol holding onto his ankles, but all he saw was blackness. At least that is what the hologram camouflage technology led the beholder to believe, there were two secret bases on the Edge of the World at both North and South Poles, accessible only if you knew how. The Government had installed the bases upon discovery that the

5

world was indeed flat. The other side of the planet was still pretty much a dark zone in terms of information about it.

In any case, this was the first of many red blobs to approach. They could hear it before they could see it clearly with the naked eye. A haunted resonating *ho, ho, ho* that echoed its way through the few trees and valleys that existed up this way, created by the ever present snowdrifts that swept their way across the surface of the North Pole.

Ho Ho Ho.

Sometimes people would wear Santa suits up here to take amusing photos and videos to send home. Nick never really understood the whole social media bullshit, though he knew that everyone else seemed to fucking love it, especially around December.

That's when the risk of people coming up this way was more prevalent. He had to ask the government to issue travel bans and the bureau of meteorology to fake inclement weather up here in the hopes of slowing down some of the Christmas time traffic, but all these warnings didn't seem to stop this fool.

After the report of something being out there from the Ops Room, Nick had grabbed one of their high-powered binoculars and gazed through the blizzard. Yep it was another one of *them*. Department store Santas, a dime a dozen; there to fleece money out of the unwilling over the Christmas period charging fifty bucks a fucking photo with good old Santa.

It wasn't even the real Santa Claus, it was just some guy that was down on his luck with a beer gut and a beard. The bastardisation was fucking endless, they even started letting women dress up as Santa Claus. What the fuck was up with that shit?

Don't get him wrong, Nick was open to anyone having a good crack at anything to make a buck, but this extended past the realms of political correctness straight into the ridiculous. Santa Claus was a dude.

Nick should know better than anyone having taken on the role of the 31st official Santa Claus two years ago.

That was a job that came out of the blue, he thought to himself, shaking his head. After the operation he wasn't allowed to talk about, The Agency had wed Nick and Carol in a secret ceremony, which they both agreed to. They had been dating for some time, having disclosed the relationship to their superiors as per the rules and guidelines set down by The Agency.

It also was easier to agree to when the Government offered to foot the wedding bill. To the rest of the world the two had eloped in Hawaii.

White Ops, Black Funds

I t was Carol that had agreed first. "You know I love skiing!" She said to him with a smile on her face when the Director discussed the opportunity to work up north.

Just how far up north, neither of them had the faintest idea but when it was mentioned that it would literally be at the top Edge of the World, Nick had his doubts. He had heard about people falling off the edge and was worried that he might do the same in a drunken stupor. There would be nothing worse than to take a tumble himself and be relegated to the nothingness that waited, but the good lady had insisted and he only existed to make her happy.

Happy wife, happy life.

Boy, oh boy, did he love his wife. A statement, not a question; Carol had saved his bacon on more than one occasion. She was funny, intelligent, attractive and damn good in the sack. He liked to think that he wasn't so bad himself and was flattered that someone he was so attracted to thought he was okay as well. She called him her Silverfox; he had gone gray early with it going through to his beard as well.

He hadn't loved the beard at first but he did like how she scratched it.

There was no beard scratching going on now, simply Nick bringing the binoculars up to his eyes and trying to get a glimpse through the blizzard for some finer detail than the red blob was providing. He gave up disgusted and handed them back to his number two, an Elf by the name of Tom Jones. Nick was pretty confident that was not his real name; in fact, most of the Elves had names of celebrities, and called each other by those names. Every now and then he would hear them speaking in their own language, which was a high speed warbling, not unlike that of a demented crow occasionally interspersed with guttural sounds that he would not have believed could come from the throats of those little people.

Tom grabbed the binoculars and raised them up to his face, adjusting the focus to assist his already keen eyes peering through them intently. He eventually dropped them in shock and awe, and turned back to Nick, who was watching him for news of what he could see.

"Hey Boss, we've really got a bad fucking problem here."

Nick hadn't seen Tom so rattled, and he'd known the Elf for nearly 2 years and trusted him implicitly. "What is it buddy?" Nick asked.

Tom picked up the binoculars and dusted off the snow and had a bit of a fiddle with the focus point. "Try looking again," he said.

Nick reached out and brought the binoculars up to his face. Of course he wanted to know what the hell that thing was that was approaching the Base. Sure, there were defense systems set up; some automated, some manually activated, however he didn't want to be smoking some drunken fuckstick, dressed up in a department store costume this close to Christmas.

It never looked good for the Agency or at least the Agency department of the North Pole a.k.a. Santa's Workshop, a.k.a. where Nick lived, a.k.a. the place that made all the kids happy.

All of a sudden he saw what it was that bothered Tom so much and he felt like vomiting. Yes it was a department store Santa dressed up in a cheap costume. You could always tell they were never as good as the real thing, and sure as fuck did not have Kevlar lining underneath. Agency protocol dictated that he always had to wear the costume when out and about in the field, just in case he was spotted by anything flying overhead. There were satellites from both domestic and foreign interests scoping the ground below as they made their way through the sky and reached the ring of beacons at the Edge of the World that stopped them from falling off into nothingness.

The thing in the distance had raised its face up just in time for Nick to see features that made his blood run cold. This guy was badly hurt. His face was a weird green, the color of mold, even under his beard that had streaks of blood running through it. Occasionally, wild animals would prey upon those who were stupid enough to wander through the snow. They got hungry, and the heat emanating from a living creature was too much for them to bear.

Some of these were wildlife that you would expect to find around these parts, wolves and the like, but of course there was no accounting for the mutated creatures that had been released around this area. To say they were failed experiments was being kind. Nick had to look after one of them about a year ago, and even to this day, he wasn't exactly sure what it was. He had dealt with a nightmarish mix of tentacles and fur. He had received a transmission warning of a wounded creature that he would have to look after, and of course being a good Agency man he'd gone out with Carol who was not a man, but his wife, of course, but also an Agent, so he guessed that made her an Agency woman. Together they would be Agency people. He shook his head. Why did his brain go off in tangents like that? He would never know.

The guy's face looked like it had been ripped off by a wild animal. It was a moldy sponge-like ribbon with chunks of rotting food left in gaping holes, like a sponge that had food left in it that had gone off. There was also something wrong with the dude's eyes, at least that's what Nick thought. The guy was still too far away, but he knew judging by the way he was limping that he would need some help. He grabbed his radio from his belt and flicked over to channel 2 which got him straight through to the Medical Center.

"Hey Med Center this is Big Poppa. We've got a problem at the outer perimeter. Some guy looks as though he's been messed up pretty badly. Take two of you out there with a stretcher, tranquilizer darts and appropriate medical equipment, expect lacerations and blood loss."

"Ten Four Big Poppa, we're on it." The response crackled back through the radio.

11

Barry White ran the Medical Center at the North Pole. An experienced veteran of urban conflict, Barry was tall enough to pass for a short human, and had served the Agency around the world in conflict areas where people simply did not like each other. The radio silenced, and about five minutes later one of the hangar doors opened, and Nick could see two Elves dressed in green uniforms, each wearing a white armband with the red cross on it shoot out the door on a snowmobile heading in the direction he had specified.

They were ridiculously efficient.

It seemed to take forever for the two to make their way to the guy. Nick wasn't sure how the man had even made it here; there were no signs of backpacks, or any other survival equipment, and you sure as hell couldn't just walk on in. It was the North Pole, damn it. Santa's workshop! You just don't just walk into the North Pole at the Edge of the World and waltz around with your face rotting off your head. An air drop sure. Well, maybe. The thing is; the skies were always clear around this part of the world, not accounting for the blizzards, and of course with the Agency's backing and the Department of Defense black ops funds being shoveled into the region as much as possible, the Elves and Nick were fully equipped with the latest in radar technology. If there was something in the sky above them, they always picked it up.

Occasionally, they did see, but not detect with radar, Unidentified Flying Objects. Nick reported these back and more often than not the Agency was aware of them, but would never say what they were. The rumor mill amongst the Elves though, was that it was the aliens. The thing they couldn't decide on was whether the aliens were from underwater or outer space. There was even talk that underneath the world, a whole alien race hid in plain sight, whilst powerful forces tricked the entire planet that the world was round so that they wouldn't look for them.

Fucking aliens. He would never have believed that aliens would ever be a part of his everyday thoughts. Except for the fact that there was one on his Base. Running the communications center no less.

The fact of the matter was that aliens were real. They did exist, and Nick had met more than one. So had Carol. Part of the deal with this gig was that you got told everything. Literally everything. The gig working in the North Pole was one of the most highly coveted and dangerous jobs in the Agency, being in such a remote location, you had to deal with all sorts of crazies. Including the extraterrestrial kind, and they weren't even crazy if he was honest with himself. Except for the time that there was an alien terrorist group in Egypt who had blown up a pyramid to create a communications tower to Hell.

One day, Nick thought he might abseil down the edge of the world and see how far he could go down before he shit himself, and beg them to haul him back up.

You All Good Bro?

T he snowmobile was almost up to the injured man, making its way through the last of the drift. The wind picked up now, the snow whirled about passing Nick's face, making it hard to breathe out. It felt as though someone was pushing breath back into his lungs as he was trying to exhale. He put his bandana over his mouth, but knew that the cold would reduce his hot breath to ice on the front of the material in a short space of time.

Everything was cold here, but that at least was something that he had gotten used to. The Agency made sure that everyone had all the latest in thermal gear, including the Elves. Why they wore it he wasn't sure as he'd seen them get drunk and run about butt ass naked in the worst blizzards with next to no signs of being cold.

Barry steered the snowmobile about twenty feet away from the limping man. From here he could smell infection; an overall reeking stench. Switching off the engine, he left the keys in and the ignition switched on. It had happened before, that the snow had fallen into the key latch and frozen up, stopping them from restarting the 'mobile. That had meant a

14

night out in a blizzard rapidly trying to build a snow wall to protect them from the cold.

The snowmobile was fitted out for survival, it came with a medical kit, tent and other basics, if someone had the dumb luck to be stuck out there. Barry motioned for Tony Bennett, his assistant, to get off the back so he could also stretch his legs. Thumping up and down on those drifts always bounced the hell out of his balls and he was keen to give himself a good shake.

Elven physiology was pretty similar to humans, hence why Barry had excelled at being a medic. Other than the fact that they were superior to humans in terms of speed and sometimes strength, hell, why not just say it the way it was? Elves were way stronger than humans and constantly needed to keep their muscles in check to keep from accidentally crushing bones when shaking hands, or breaking things that humans made. That was why, when The Agency developed the North Pole Toy Shop, the Elves were a natural fit. Naturally hardy and seemingly impervious to the freezing cold.

It was crazy though, Barry thought. He'd been at the North Pole for quite some time now, only occasionally having been ordered by The Agency to work further afield. Elves could handle the heat, they just didn't like it. But Barry was a professional and went where he was told. He motioned for Tony to go forward and check the guy out. Tony grunted and got off the snowmobile properly this time doing a quick stretch before grabbing a medical kit. Tony's nose prickled and he turned back to Barry and said,

"There's no way this can go well. Can you fucking smell him?"

Barry nodded, "Be super careful, that's a really bad smell and I don't like the way he's walking. Fucking humans, why do they always come up to these places where they have no chance of walking back out alive again?"

He thought for a second and quickly added, "Hey Tony, are you packing?"

Tony nodded and patted his right side, lifting up the top of his coat to show a holstered service issue Glock. "Yes Boss. Locked and loaded. Give me a second, and I'll check this fucker out."

Barry grabbed out the radio again and let Nick know that they were approaching the putrid asshole tourist. He looked back. In the distance, he could see the boss standing there with binoculars raised, Tom beside him. For a human, Nick was a good sort and always made sure he was checking on the welfare of all the guys. Barry was pretty confident that occasionally Nick was overwhelmed, but he had managed to do a good job nonetheless for the last two years. They all made a pretty good team with very few upsets.

The radio issued a lot of static which was common, but Barry could sense Nick understood what he was saying. Interference with communications was an issue up in these regions. There were so many weird things around this part of the world that it could even be the aliens transmitting to each other. Yes, Barry had met them, more than once. He didn't like them or trust them. They were secretive and didn't talk a lot except for the one guy back at the North Pole who helped

16

them out with communications and radar. That guy, Mike the Alien, God that guy could drink.

He returned his attention back to Tony and got the medical stuff ready, including the stretcher. There was no way this guy was gonna be able to walk back and there wasn't enough room on the snowmobile. Essentially the stretcher was a modified sled which could be comfortably towed behind the snowmobile without having snow kicked up and all over the patient. It had been used before primarily in training and also on more than one occasion when Nick had decided to get hammered and go for a walk at night. They were just lucky that the GPS built to his suit had activated the perimeter alarms before he had stumbled off the Edge of the World.

Barry had absolutely no idea why they decided to build this place so close to the Edge, but that was how it was. It was obviously above his pay grade. He guessed it made sense from a defense perspective to make this place as hard as possible to get to, but it also did mean that they were surrounded by what he would call monsters, and also being occasionally buzz bombed by the aliens as they flew to and fro. For some reason, the aliens really liked entering the world from around here. It must have something to do with the magnetic fields, or maybe they simply could slip in undetected through all the satellites already hovering in the area, jamming up radar and other communications.

Tony approached the guy apprehensively, the rancid stench was almost too much. The closer he got, the more he could smell the rot and hear that weird laughing sound it was making. He had trouble calling this thing a he, even though it was clearly a dude. It had a weird, gurgling, laugh.

"Ho, ho, ho"

It was as though there was a frog caught inside its throat in a pond filled with shit.

"Hey buddy, I'm here to help." Tony said.

He could tell from this distance that this was a cheap Santa suit on the guy with nothing underneath to keep him safe from the hail and cold. Icicles had formed on the guy's motley green face, blood was all over him, not just little specks, but great puddles like the guy had tried and failed in a game of paintball.

This guy had been severely fucked up and Tony had no idea how he was still on his feet. The human looked up and all the blood drained from Tony's face as he realized just how much damage had been inflicted to this cheap Santa. An eye was missing, there were deep lacerations exposing cheekbone, and part of the guy's jaw had been ripped off, exposing blackened teeth inside the mouth which hung weirdly from skin that was clearly rotting. At this distance, the stench was like week-old tuna oil mixed in with diapers, then garnished with mustard and left in the sun, then spread out onto a raw sashimi dish garnished in a floating bed of curdled milk.

"What the fuck?!" He knew that something was desperately wrong and at this point, there was nothing to do for the guy, there was no possible way a man could survive these injuries, taking the sickening stench into account. By all means this man….. was already dead, at least as far as Tony was concerned. The Santa looked up and with its good eye focused squarely on him, the shambling increased and Tony backed up in horror.

18

"Ho, ho ho. Ho, ho, ho."

For a second there, as the guy's arms came up, Tony thought maybe it was a plea for help and he paused, but then he noticed the insects coming out of the Santa's mouth and stumbled backwards, flailing. The Santa cleared the distance between them quickly, and Tony scrambled backwards trying to grab his pistol out of his holster. The guy's fingers closed around his leg, managing to break through the snow suit with bony finger tips, puncturing Tony's leg.

There was an intensity born of hunger behind the dead guy's dead white eye that stared at him as the jawbone swung in the wind as the Santa slowly clawed its way up Tony's body. Tony finally managed to get the gun from his holster and squeezed off a couple of shots. One hit the guy on the side of the face. The other was square in his chest, and the other one which bucked a little bit wide, shattered through the shoulder joint attached to the arm that was clamped through his leg.

The Santa's grip went limp, which gave him respite, but to Tony's shock, the Santa kept on coming. With resolution, Tony emptied the rest of the clip into the guy, square in the center mass. It should've been enough to drop any human, some Elves would've been able to withstand it, but at this range, even they would have struggled to live, but the Santa kept on coming and raised his good arm. Tony kicked out and the Santa's hand that was stabbed through his thigh ripped loose and its skin tore and stretched apart, yet the guy showed no pain or discomfort at suddenly becoming dismembered.

Tony, with no ammunition left, swept the pistol around and whipped the guy in the head. He heard the skull break, but to no avail. There was a brief pause and the Santa kept on coming, grabbing Tony's hand that was holding the weapon and closing its broken jaw around it. Lowering its head it tore a good chunk of flesh from Tony's hand and he screamed with the pain. The sheer agony was incredible, and he looked at the dangling flesh from his own body hanging out of this thing's mouth as it chewed and maintained its grip on him.

In the distance, so close, yet so far away, Barry watched all this unfold. He saw Tony empty an entire fucking magazine into the Santa which did not slow it down. He'd never expected something with so many deadly wounds to have attacked. It took him by surprise; in all his years with The Agency he had never seen anything quite like this, then to his horror he saw the thing fucking chomp on Tony and start ripping him apart. There was no point shooting except in one direction.

The Santa had ripped most of Tony's cheek away with its broken fingers, and was devouring the flesh in a lazy, almost luxurious fashion. There were multiple lacerations all over Tony's body, all of which were immediately infecting him and overpowering his natural ability to heal quickly. The fact that a human could do this to an Elf took Barry by surprise, and he just knew that Tony was fucked. All he could do now from this distance was a mercy killing. He raised his weapon and fired three shots into Tony who slumped down with the creature in a hideous deathly embrace.

Barry just hoped his pal was dead. The Santa kept eating Tony for a short while until it noticed Barry as it tore more flesh from its kill then got up and started shambling toward him, going over Tony's body as it did so.

The radio crackled and Barry could hear Nick, even through the static. His message was clear.

"Get the fuck out of there, there's nothing you can do, just get the fuck out of there. What the fuck is that thing! Barry, do you hear me! Get the fuck out of there right now. That's a direct order!"

The Santa shambled forward as Barry stumbled onto the snowmobile. He feverishly pushed the button to get it started up. Somehow he'd knocked the ignition into the off position during the attack on Tony. The damn thing had sealed over as snow had melted then refrozen. He needed to break it, or he'd be next. Sure, he could outrun the thing he thought at least for a time. It wasn't fast, but in this blizzard there was just as much chance of him falling and hurting himself and then getting caught, as there was him getting away.

He reached into the satchel that was around his waist, and his fingers closed on something round and metallic. Perfect. He pulled the frag grenade out and bashed it against the ice stopping the ignition button from being pushed down and starting the snowmobile. The ice cracked, and he finally got the button depressed, and the 'mobile roared to life vibrating below him. He looked down at the grenade and at the thing that had just killed his friend. Anger consumed him as the Santa made its way closer like an unstoppable force. Barry's finger curled around the pin, his knuckles turning white.

"You. Cunt."

Barry pulled the pin on the grenade and lobbed it at the Santa, gunning the engine as he did. He had three seconds to get the fuck out of there before the fuse detonated and wasted them both. The engine on the snowmobile revved high toward the redline and slammed forward with force, lifting the front skis into the air briefly. In a panic, Barry thought that the damn thing would flip, trapping him underneath it as the grenade was going to go off, but at the last moment the skis bit and it sped forward making him hold on for dear life as the strength of the engine threatened to throw him backwards.

The grenade exploded, sending its fragments through the cold air and shredding the Santa to pieces. It fell face forward into the snow with the top half of its head missing. Splatters of green mold, blood, and yellow gore flew across the white of the snow like one of those paintings they try to convince you is fine art when all that has happened is the artist has flicked random colors at a canvas. He turned back around to the snowmobile's controls and sped back to Base. What the fuck had just happened? All of a sudden he needed a drink.

A really strong one.

Video

The operations room was packed and filled with excited chatter. Nick sat at the head of the table with Carol at the other end, and together they swiveled their chairs and watched the huge screen on the wall across from them. The Elves all sat about in attendance as one of the video technicians manipulated and cleared up the footage from Barry's body cam. It would have been helpful to have actually got the footage from Tony but there was no way at this current time.

They weren't going out there to even try to retrieve Tony without any idea of what the fuck they were dealing with, and why that *thing* was even in the area in the first place. Barry sat next to Nick with a glass of scotch poured neat. Mike the Alien had seen to that as soon as he saw his friend had returned to Toy Base.

As they waited for the video to start properly, Barry turned to Nick.

"I'm so sorry Boss. I'm sorry I couldn't help Tony. It was really fucked up, I should've been there for him, it's all my fault."

Nick looked down at his friend, compassion filling his face.

"Brother, that's fucking bullshit, and you know it. None of us could've expected what happened to actually happen. That… thing should've been dead on the ground. It was hit so many times and kept on coming. That's not normal, it's not natural, and we need to get to the fucking bottom of this. I'm really sorry about Tony, we all are but it's not your fault. So don't focus on that, he would want you to focus on what we can do to work out what the fuck this is and what we do about it."

Carol got up from her chair and walked around to Barry, placing an arm around his shoulder and patting his hand with the other. He rested his cheek against her arm briefly as she signaled for the video to play.

The body cam footage was surprisingly clear with not a lot of augmentation required. The technician was able to zoom in on the attack which took place in a matter of seconds, though Nick was sure that to Tony, it seemed like it took forever. The most troubling thing, other than the sounds of the gunfire, and the weird laughter the thing was making, was the fact that they could all hear Barry's panicked breathing, which made the whole thing seem even more real, even in the safe confines of headquarters. The experienced combat medic was terrified and the camera recorded that as dispassionately as it had the tearing apart of Tony.

"Zoom in on its face," Nick said and the technician stopped the video and zoomed in on the Santa's face.

24

It was ripped to shreds and absolutely rotten. It was clear to everyone not affected by the heat of the moment that this thing was dead and still moving. Its face was devoid of expression other than a weird look that it took once it realized that Tony was in front of it. The expression was hunger. They watched the rest of the video in silence, with several of the Elves covering their eyes, and even hardened veterans of multiple conflicts briefly looking away as their friend was torn to shreds by broken teeth and shredded fingers.

A word kept coming to the surface of Nick's mind, but he didn't want to say it out loud. If he did, he was sure that even in this environment he would be mocked.

"Zombie. That's a fucking zombie."

The entire table turned to look at Carol. The room went quiet as she stared back at all of them in defiance.

"Yes, you all heard what I said, and I fucking meant it. That was a zombie like in the fucking movies, what else shambles along and is so obviously fucking dead, and despite the fact that Tony put an entire magazine into this fucking thing, it still kept on coming and fucked him up, and our friend is dead. A fucking zombie. In fact, the only thing that even stops it is the fact that Barry threw a friggin grenade that blew it to bits."

Carol settled back into her chair and took a sip of her tea. It was rapidly cooling down on the table in front of her. One of the elves pulled out a flask of whiskey and offered it to her and she dumped half of the contents in and handed it back. Taking a sip, she grimaced in disgust. Then gulped down the rest of the cup and put it in front of her.

25

"Look at the footage. The thing only stops when the top of its head has been blown off. Like in the movies, let's not make any bones about that. It's not until there is brain death that it even looks as though it's going to stop."

Nick turned to his wife. As always, she had spoken the words that he was thinking. "Honey, are you sure? Zombies?"

She turned to him and said, "Sweetheart, ever since we took on this job, we've seen so much weird shit that we would never have imagined was even real, including these guys."

She gestured around the room at all the Elves and Mike the Alien. "Sorry guys, by weird shit I didn't mean you're weird, I simply mean stuff that normal humans don't get to see on the daily." She got up and started pacing the room.

"So yes, let's assume that these things are fucking zombies. We have Elves, aliens and a secret base under the North Pole on the other side of the planet, so I don't think zombies are out of the question at this point. Do you? And let's not forget our furry friends in the stables."

There was a pause. Well, everyone stopped and considered her words. What were the ramifications for the Base? This was something none of them had ever encountered.

Nick spoke up, "Hey Mike the Alien, you were in Ops about the time we ran into that... zombie" Mike the Alien nodded and took in a breath.

"Guys before we go to that information, there was something on that video you probably didn't see. Yes, it's an alien thing before you ask, but I've managed to isolate some of Barry's footage. Just here, as the grenade is going off. I'll

26

zoom in for you and enhance." Mike the Alien pushed buttons on his keyboard and the room gasped. There, behind the Santa, just as the grenade detonated….. was Tony. On his feet. And very very dead. Then the grenade went off and tore the two apart.

Mike the Alien looked Barry straight in the eyes. "I reiterate bro, Tony is already dead before that grenade goes off. This is not on you. The bites of this thing did that." Barry nodded in gratitude and the table turned back to Nick.

Nick went on. "Did anything else happen as far as you guys could pick up around the same time? I know you're probably wondering why I ask, but the way that guy was dressed. Correction, zombie was dressed, there's no way it just came in here by itself."

Mike the Alien flipped up the lid of his laptop, and with a specially modified keyboard for his three fingers, rapidly brought up the data requested. *Not a bad guy for an alien*, Nick thought. Mike the Alien had been with the firm for a while now, not as long as Mike the Elf of course, and while some of the Elves had problems with the aliens, Nick had found them to be on the up and up for the most part.

It wouldn't surprise me if they had their own agenda, he thought to himself. *But let's face it, fucking everyone does*. At the end of the day, Mike the Alien had treated him with dignity and respect since day one, and Nick and Carol both had learnt little parts of Mike the Alien's language to return the favor.

It wasn't as complex as people would think; mainly a matter of modifying how your tongue shaped sounds. Mike the Alien had told them that his true speech was a mixture of audio and telepathy, but Nick was not willing to have the brain surgery Mike the Alien offered in order to do it. There were a lot of similarities to human speech, enough that occasionally, Mike the Alien would laugh out loud when Nick yelled obscenities across the room at him. It was always the first thing people learnt when studying another language; swear words.

"Oh, yes. Here we go." Mike the Alien tapped thoughtfully on the screen and turned it around so that both Mike and Carol could see properly. He had brought up the radar data which was constantly being recorded, and pretty easy for anyone to follow. It was the fine tuning of these things during blizzards and other electrical interferences that was Mike the Alien's specialty. Otherwise, for the most part, all the Elves and even Nick and Carol were able to figure out the more generic radar data.

"Okay, so the space is relatively clear for most of the day, as you can see, but then when Tony gets jumped…" Mike the Alien fiddled around with the keyboard, and then transmitted the image of the radar to the big screen in the Ops room. They all turned to look at that instead of squinting at the smaller laptop screen. Carol could see the usual swirling motion of the radar, then all of a sudden an almost indistinguishable blip appeared near the Edge of the World close enough to drop something off near their Base, but far enough away to be confused with all the junk that was accumulating up in that airspace.

"That's a decent size transport plane by the looks of things," Mike the Alien said. "I was thinking about this earlier, and considering the fact that thing gets pumped full of bullets and keeps on trucking, that maybe, just maybe this

Santa… zombie was airdropped in." There were audible gasps around the room as this information was absorbed.

This sort of thing was so hard to grasp. It was as though it had been ripped from the pages of a short novel written by an unknown author, who had tried to put every conspiracy theory known to man into the one book. The ramifications of an airdropped Undead Santa was preposterous to say the least, but in this world, not improbable. Action had to be taken and fast. At the very least Nick needed to let The Agency know what they may be up against.

He turned to Justin, also known as JT, an Elf who operated the communications board in the Ops room. "Get me the Director please JT, immediately." The room fell silent as the call was connected as a priority and within a few minutes, the Director of The Agency appeared on the screen. His normally friendly relaxed face was serious. "Hi Nick, what's up? Oh hey Carol, hi everyone." The Director took in the room, full of pale faced humans, Elves, and of course Mike the Alien whose gray face was a lighter shade than normal.

"Hey Calvin, we're all good here. Actually, we're not good at all. That's why the priority comm. I've sent through some video footage to you. Can you have a quick look at this? Please see what you can think about it? In fact, if you have anyone else there, get them to look at it with you. We've lost one of our people to this thing and I thought I should give you the heads up. Mike the Alien is under the opinion that this thing was dropped in by transport plane and if that's the case, they may know exactly what we do here in the Toy Shop or at least what's underneath the main hanger."

They all watched as the director summoned over three of his lackeys in the situation room, and quietly they watched the video that Nick had sent through. The audio of the attack, coming back through the microphone in the Directors office sounded both teeny and horrific at the same time. Everyone at Nick's end knew exactly what the fuck had happened, and what sounds were being made at which time. Finally, they heard the thud of Barry's frag grenade, and the Director looked back up at the camera. The men watching the video with him, quickly whispered in his ear, looked at each other and nodded. Then letting out a long breath, the Director prepared to speak.

"Nick, thanks for sending this through. We had a bad feeling something like this would occur one day. In fact, we were about to contact you with a warning, based on Intel gathered from our European connection. Looks like the bad guys beat us to it. Multiple transport planes have been spotted, heading over key parts of the world. The transponders don't seem to conform to any known standards. We have a bad feeling that -"

The audio started cutting out and static filled the screen cutting off the connection with the Director. The screen flickered and then the connection died entirely and so did their contact with the outside world.

Jingle Bell Rot

There was a heavy humming noise directly above them that made the thick concrete walls of the Toy Shop vibrate slightly and Nick looked up at the ceiling waiting for it to fall in on him. The sound was that ominous that some of the Elves had already climbed under tables. He looked at Carol who had a concerned expression on her face. "This can't be good love," she said. The doors burst open giving everyone a fright. Mark, the Elf in charge of the Ops room when Mike the Alien wasn't there rushed in with a printout in his hand and said, "Boss we have company. A lot of company. It appeared out of nowhere. Quick, you have to see this."

Nick grabbed Carol's hand, and together they raced through the corridors of the Base, briefly passing the locked door that led down to an area that they had never been to, and were given orders that under no circumstances were they to go there unless specifically directed. Most people avoided this part of the Toy Shop preferring to go the long way on the eastern wing. They ran past a steady stream of worried faces waiting for Nick to give them direction. Gradually the corridor sloped upward to the outer doors, which were slowly opening to allow them access, their heavy, bombproof mechanisms making the process torturous. The two squeezed through the opening with the Elves close behind them and looked skyward. There, just lower than the clouds were the silhouettes of at least thirty large transport planes making their way through the sky. Directly over the Toy Shop.

"Are the fucking shields up?" Nick asked out loud. "No," said Enrique. "Then get them the fuck up," Nick yelled. A button was punched on an emergency panel and a forcefield dome enclosed the Toy Shop, and the surrounding wilderness. The lights inside the Base dimmed briefly, then corrected themselves.

The shields used so much power that they were rarely turned on. The normal generators just didn't have the strength to maintain so much energy for a prolonged period of time. Nick looked up and marveled. The shields being activated was something that he never got sick of seeing. So much power with the ability to repel most objects and certainly most attacks. The electrical shield was generated by transmitters placed around the grounds with roughly a mile radius beyond the actual Toy Shop. It was like something out of a fucking science-fiction movie. And to be honest, one day after quite a few drinks, about fifteen of them went outside, activated the shields and shot things at them, laughing as bullets bounced off the surface or melted entirely. One of the guys even tried peeing on it and the stream didn't even make it to the forcefield before evaporating.

Nick felt fairly confident the shield would protect them for at least the foreseeable future, and if any more of those fucking zombies were being dropped off, then they would have well over a mile of distance to cover before they came anywhere near the Toy Shop and the amazing secrets it kept on its grounds.

A new sound gradually permeated its way over the drone of the engines as the planes crawled their way overhead. It was the sound of bells ringing. The direction they were taking was parallel to the Edge of the World, *so obviously the pilots knew about that little humdinger,* Nick thought. Squinting, he looked up, and he could see massive church bells attached to the bottom of each of the planes, clanging and clattering as they made their way through the sky. A cacophony of sound rattled back down to Earth as loudspeakers played cheerful music from the aircraft in a disjointed fashion. It sounded like thirty preschoolers had been given bells and were told to shake them in time to the same song; it just did not happen.

Nick looked around and so far, everything seemed peaceful enough around the Toy Shop. He picked up his radio and spoke to Lenny, the elf in charge of toy manufacture. "Hey Lenny? Everything okay there?" He could hear the hustle and bustle in the Toy Shop as the Elves were getting things ready for the Christmas flyover. Yes, even with all the other side agendas the cover story would never be blown and so therefore, every Christmas Santa's Toy Shop roared to life making toys for kids all over the entire world.

This operation had been started by the Department of Defense so far back no one really knew how it all started. Nick thought the Elves probably did. They lived to an insane age compared to human standards, and most of them remembered the very first Agent who had been sent to the North Pole. Humans were but blinks in their existence, which was why a lot of the Elves simply called him Boss. They simply could not keep up, and he was sure that most humans looked the same to them for the most part. Reassuringly though, they all took a liking to Carol. it was almost impossible not to, and he would often hear them cheerfully calling out to her, referring to her as either the Mrs or Mrs Carol.

It kind of made sense really why the Agency only staffed the Toy Shop with Elves. Even Mike the Alien was a new addition by comparison. He had been sent up from Roswell a long time ago after his craft was recovered by humans. When his buddies had arrived en masse, he had chosen to stay with humanity. He would occasionally get teleported out for a few hours every now and then, mentioning something about a family. Nick hoped it was to at least see them sometimes. At least for a quick conjugal.

Lenny answered in the affirmative. The Toy Shop was up and running smoothly with production not being affected. The temporary loss of power had not impacted production whatsoever. Nick told him to keep on truckin' and switched off.

Carol heard the conversation as it came through the radio and Nick asked her, "Do you think they're here for the toys?"

Her face softened as she realized he was serious, she held his hand, looked into his eyes and said words that chilled him to the core.

"No my love. They're here for the nukes."

Red Death

As if on cue, the planes all simultaneously dipped lower but out of range of the forcefield and red bodies begin to drop to earth. Thousands of them plummeted down like a flesh rainstorm, and all through the air one noise erupted through thousands of mouths.

"Ho. Ho. Ho."

The Zombie Claus Cometh

T he fucking nukes! Nick knew he had overlooked something. He'd been that caught up in the Christmas rush, and the trip that he was meant to be making this evening that he had totally forgotten the fucking stockpile hidden underneath the Toy Shop. In fact, it was the main reason the Toy Shop even existed. The biggest arsenal that the Department of Defense had ever amassed of nuclear weapons; they partially powered this place and also made sure that no one would fuck with the free world. For God's sake, it was one of the first things that they actually told you when you took over the Toy Shop; nukes are underneath.

"Oh, crap, I'm sorry my sweet, I totally forgot about them!" Carol looked at him and said, "That's okay dear, we've got a little bit of time to figure this out first. How about you give the order for battle stations?" Nick grabbed the alert button that dangled around his neck. He popped the top off, pressed the button and Klaxon sirens sounded from every mounted speaker.

"Alert, alert, alert. Elves to stations, Elves to stations." He could hear hundreds of little footsteps running throughout the Toy Shop. In fact, the entire Base was now on alert and ready. Nick and Carol went back inside and could see the sergeant at arms handing out assault rifles to Elves as they quickly kitted up for combat. They were prepared for this and Nick felt a touch of pride. Yes, he had forgotten about the damn nuclear weapons, but drills and training were something that he did encourage, and made sure that multiple times a week everyone, himself included, was ready for an unexpected attack. He never thought it would happen, but now this is what they were faced with.

He and Carol went into the tea room, where his most trusted leaders waited for his word. He grabbed a mug of coffee, took a sip and said, "Alright guys, this one looks serious. In fact, I would go so far as to say this is a great deal worse than the Abominable attack we experienced fifteen months ago. And we all know that was bad. RIP Mariah."

They all quickly bowed their heads. "We need to get on top of this, and quickly folks. You have to know that headshots are all that will work. We need to destroy those fuckers from the neck upwards and by that I mean the very top of the head. I hate to say it, these are zombies, no question about it, and if the movies stand to any rhyme or reason whatsoever it's going to be the death of the brain that does the job."

He took a pause and continued.

"I'm not gonna lie, the situation is utterly fucked. There are a metric shit ton of those monsters out there, but unfortunately they have all fallen out of range of the 'shield, so only a few got vaporized in the fall. So to pull a good thing out of this shit storm, at least we got that thing up in time. Get your boys, get out there, and make sure we keep talking to each other. Bobby?" Nick looked at one of the team leaders, tying a red band around his arm. Bobby looked up, "Yeah Boss?"

"Take your Team and disperse them to all the outer perimeter stations. I need Intel and quick, we've seen one of them. I'm guessing this is more of the same, but just in case, I want eyes on the ground. Go right now. The rest of you, get your Teams and get them prepared in five minutes tops, then get your asses back to the Ops room so that we can see just what the fuck we're dealing with."

Sit, Rep

The atmosphere in the Ops room was tense. Quiet voices chatted. The Elves for the sake of speed spoke in their own language switching to English whenever Nick or Carol came nearby. Nick had picked up a little bit of Elf, enough to know they were saying things were not great. But he also saw the determination on their faces and knew that he had the right team here. Not that he had any say in the damn thing; they had been here for a long time before him, and chances were, they would all be here after he was long gone. It was moments like these he wished he'd taken that plum post in Miami. At least it would've been warm. He shook his head, a wry smile on his face. There was no way he would want to be anywhere but here with his beautiful wife and these good people. *People*, what a generic word for the mix he was looking at. He wouldn't have it any other way.

Bobby was on camera now, on the main screen, his face worried as he held his high-powered camera to his own face so that they could see him. Nick nodded, and activated their camera. "What have you got there? Bobby?"

"You are right Boss, things are messed up. There are thousands of the fuckers all around the place. They're about half a mile away from the shield. That should give us enough time to get some things in place here, but I'd strongly suggest using heavier armaments as well. There are way more of them than us, but with the right explosives, we should be able to send most of them to Kingdom Come well before they even approach. Some of them are a bit too close for comfort, we've been tracking them for a short period of time. Here is the footage live right now."

Bobby turned the camera back around and zoomed in. The Ops room could all see a whole bunch of department store Santa zombies, staggering their way through the forest. Every now and then one would fall in a hole under the snow, or trip, discharging the weapons that they all seemed to be holding. Even at this distance, Nick could not figure out why they had been armed; none seemed to be able to work their rifles. Maybe whoever had sent them was just hoping for accidental damage through weapon discharge. He had no idea.

All of the zombies had suffered damage being thrown out of the planes, but surprisingly, most of them were mobile. Some got tangled up in each other and others were in trees. Others simply used their arms to pull their bodies along as their legs were shattered or just missing entirely. It was a crazy sight, one that he wouldn't soon forget. And once again, that horrible ho, ho, ho. He had no idea how they were making that noise. In most of the movies he had seen, zombies made a growling noise, or a hungry sound, or a wheezy, I've just had fifteen cigarettes in a row kind of noise and now I can't breathe, and I will have emphysema in about thirty years kind of sound. Not this horrible, guttural laughter. He felt sorry for whoever had to genetically modify the throats of these things to produce that noise. Surely the work of a mad scientist?

Mad Science

==

The Agency had come up against mad scientists before, this was nothing new. They were all over the world, making their weapons of mass destruction, and generally having fun with DNA strands and gene splicing. The Agency for the most part let them work their macabre magic in the off chance that they actually produced something worth using.

Sometimes that got out of control, and a team was sent in to wipe the scientist and their works off the face of the Flat Earth. They kept popping up though, like cockroaches; one soon taking the place of the other, taking greater risks as they thought their work went undetected. Of course The Agency knew about most of them, but it was the weird and arcane that sometimes slipped past them as they simply thought the idea was too kooky to even follow up. It seemed to be the case this time too; who the fuck would've thought that someone would make zombies? Let alone dress them all up like Santa. Nick looked down at his red combat suit. Like him.

But yet, that was what he was faced with. Damn zombies. He remembered enjoying the movies as a kid and thought this

42

would never happen in real life but of course, here we are. Fantasy becomes reality once again.

The radio crackled, interrupting his train of thought. He pushed the button to talk, and said, "Yes Bobby?"

There was a pause, so he could hear breathing on the other end of the line. It sounded as though Bobby was out of breath. The camera was covered so all he could hear was the audio, but then the darkness lifted from the visual and Bobby was visible. Behind him a group of Elves struggled to contain something writhing around. "Boss, I thought you might be interested to know this. We caught one."

Under the Hood

The Med Bay was packed with onlookers. Nick couldn't blame them. He too was interested, but at least he had the right to have front row seats along with Carol as the doctor poked and prodded the heavily restrained Santa zombie on the gurney. As the doctor cut away the Santa suit with a set of heavy shears, she spoke out loud into the recorder that was dangling above her station, and also to Nick directly. Every now and then, an expletive in Elvish erupted from her lips. This was something that she had never come across in her long life. Barry helped as best he could. This was well above his medic paygrade.

Getting out an angle grinder, of course of the medical kind, the doc cut through the rib cage. There was a cracking noise and a lot of gas that escaped from the cavity making even the more experienced attendees gasp at such a horrible stench. However, interestingly enough, no blood or gore erupted from the openings.

"Okay Boss, I'm gonna go through this very quickly, and we don't really have a lot of time here I get that, but we may uncover something within this thing's body that helps us. As you can see right now it is still animated, even though there has been no response to pain. We have secured the head and limbs with titanium bands. It isn't going anywhere. Barry, be careful of the teeth. We saw what happened to Tony. We don't need to repeat that experience. So as I was saying there's a lack of vital signs, and the most obvious observation is the absence of normal life as we understand it with this creature. Normally, we would be seeing a heartbeat, respiration, and of course body temperature. There is none of this here, yet the thing still moves. Look closely at the flesh."

She pulled back a peeling rotten hunk of skin from the chest and continued. "We are seeing advanced decomposition with rotting flesh, discolored skin, and of course a putrid odor. This may be from the presence of food, namely meat inside the gullet, but we are also convinced that this is because of the internal organs failing and rotting. Atrophy would eventually occur naturally, once enough rot takes hold in the corpse. The creature does seem to pull nutrients from its food source, however, decomposition is overtaking it faster than it could ever possibly sustain itself. A natural death, or the inability for the creature to have locomotion would typically be seen after one to six months. This is not to say that it wouldn't have animation about its face and teeth; the killing part of its body. We can't forget this is an eating machine and what remains of brain function as such will all be about eating until the brain is destroyed, and that signal is stopped."

The doctor moved more of the Santa suit away and noticed damage on the torso. "This is very interesting. It looks as though this is not the first time that this particular creature has been in contact with other lifeforms. See here?" She pointed. "This is from a blade being wielded. These creatures may have been tested against other human subjects in a real life combat environment. Obviously it has survived as its victims did not realize the best way to get rid of the menace."

She went further, "Even now, all that this creature is focused on is food and destruction. This intense focus is primarily controlled visually, and whilst it lasts, its sense of smell. I would like to now demonstrate what happens if the creature loses sight."

She got a scalpel out, and being careful to avoid the moving head even though its teeth were bound, skilfully cut out and removed with a gloved hand, the zombie's right eye. Its movement ceased almost immediately, as it could no longer see anything from that side. There were no utterings of pain, and no blood, other than a gentle oozing from the wound.

"One thing that we do need to work out is why the zombies are coming back toward the Base. From our quick analysis here, along with the video provided from Barry's bodycam, we can see that these things are motivated by their never ending hunger for the living. They show no interest in environmental stimuli, even when it comes to sources of pain. We can only surmise that potentially there is something or someone controlling their movement, or in fact, that it is the presence of our shield and the energy humming from it that is attracting them. Electricity is generated by our bodies to a far lesser extent, however, the presence of something so high-powered may be like a beacon in the night to them. In fact, as we know, the shield emanates a loud humming noise. That would also send vibrations through the nearby environment."

She paused to let that sink in. "We can't turn off the shield, that much is obvious. However, it's good to know what these things are attracted to. Finally though, this is just for cursory reasons and for me to log this in case it is needed elsewhere, I have tested for reflexes and other than visual motivation, it has none. Or at least none of the normal human or Elven areas of physiological response that I have checked. Knee tapping affects nothing, nor do any explorations of usual pressure points on the human body; it is indeed a conundrum as the creature is both dead and alive at the same time. Last, but not least, please step back."

She went to a stainless steel table and grabbed a surgical pick and mallet. "Everyone in the room take a step back please and don masks," she said. "I am extremely certain that whatever virus this thing has can be spread via blood through direct contact or airborne inhalation." They all tightened their masks and took a step back. The doctor lowered her goggles and placed the tip of the ice pick against the Santa zombie's head. "We know that brain death will stop all bodily function, however allow me to demonstrate just where you will need to attack."

She placed the icepick over the remaining eye on the zombie and smashed down with determination. The pick cracked through the back of the socket, squishing the eyeball around it, yet the zombie kept on moving now utterly blind. "As you can see, lower brain injury doesn't seem to do much does it? We do need to make sure it's in the top half of the brain or that the brain itself is severed via the cord from the rest of the body. Far easier to aim for upper head shots or complete immolation of the brain through blunt force, trauma or explosive." For good effect, she punctured the head of the creature multiple times, with no change to its behavior. Finally finishing in the upper half, she drove the pick through the skull puncturing the top of the brain. The zombie slumped unmoving on the gurney, and the doctor stepped back to place the pick and the mallet into a nearby tray.

"Upper brain death is what we need. Upper brain death will be the only thing to stop these things, we can't risk even dismembering and leaving a body in the snow. Heaven knows how long it will last and what creatures it may come across in that time. Think of it as a landmine of sorts, just waiting for someone to step on it."

She turned away, and went back to scrubbing her hands as the nurses unbound the body and sent it away for incineration.

"Nick, for what it's worth, I took samples before this demonstration of blood, skin and other substances. Those have been sent to the lab but if you don't stop the army outside, I guess it really won't matter. Tell everyone to make sure they're wearing masks even if they find it uncomfortable. The last thing you want is to hit one of these things and have its blood go into your mouth. I do think that would fuck you up good and quick. We don't have time to test this, however let's face it, this is the stuff of science-fiction so we may as well play by those rules for now until we know better."

A computer generated voice chimed in from the speakers above.

~ One hour until the zombie horde reaches the shield. Six hours until Christmas day. Have a festive day ~

"So honey, what do you think?" Nick asked Carol. She put her hands on her hips and stared back at him. "I think the situation is fucked to be honest sweetheart, but really there's nothing in all of our training that would cover this. The fucking Undead, who would've thought on Christmas Eve instead of loading the sleigh we'd be loading up assault rifles? So we've got an hour huh? I think it's time we let the Dirty Dozen in on what's going on."

Fur O'cious

"Really?" Nick thought out aloud. The Dirty Dozen was the codename for the reindeer in the stables. They had arrived even before the Elves at the North Pole. No one knew their origins, and even though they had mastered human speech, they would not say where they were from. They had always been friends of The Agency, and more importantly they actually seemed very focused on their job of getting presents all around the world on one special night in the year.

Everyone at The Toy Shop totally bought into the mission and its cover story, and in some cases, more research and development funds were spent on toys than the actual weapons they were meant to be developing. The argument was that most toys could be reverse engineered into making something that could kill another human and sometimes that was actually true. It was more that the whole message of cheer and joy was infectious, and the reindeer were keen to play their part, as were the Elves.

In fact, even cynical Nick had been sucked in by all the letters they received. Postal services around the world did deliver letters written to Santa directly to the North Pole, and that first year he just binned them (something he was more than a little ashamed of). Nick hated paperwork, but eventually curiosity had gotten the better of him and he had started reading them. They captured both his heart and his imagination, and sucked him in despite the fact that he knew ultimately he could do very little about most of them.

"Okay, the Dirty Dozen it is," he said. "Get them out as quickly as possible. In fact, tell them to come out right now on the radio. I think that Rudolph has cones on, and let them know to meet me outside in the quadrangle ASAP. R&D? (Research & Development) Do we have the harnesses that we made six months ago? Yes? Great, they were field tested, yeah?" One of the elves nodded. "Yes Boss, fully tested, field checked and pretty accurate on my data pad here considering the fact that the launch system is unconventional to say the least."

Nick stroked his beard thoughtfully. "That's fine, go get them and get me twenty-four missiles with low yield warheads. We don't want to blow this fucking place up with a misfire." Everyone murmured their agreement. Nick didn't like using the reindeer for this purpose. He had field tested them in combat. They were surprisingly good at it, but at the same time they were an integral part of the rest of the cover story, so skillfully painted many moons ago.

He and Carol made their way back out to the quadrangle where the last of the reindeer had landed, and were waiting for their briefing. Yet another one of the mysteries of the North Pole was that there were twelve flying reindeer here. A previous Santa had logged the appearance of four new reindeer roughly 100 years ago. All Santa files had been digitized and stored on the central mainframe for ready access and use. All the records said was that the initial eight reindeer had one day disappeared during the summer months. As was their habit. It was assumed on vacation; they never said where they went. The reindeer were secretive yet loyal, but they came back with four new friends who had stayed ever since.

One of them, a young reindeer with a bright red nose, had made the mistake of getting too close to humans and forming part of mythology. In fact, having a song named after him as well as being attributed with the wrong name. The four new reindeer names were actually Michelangelo, Donatello, Raphael and Leonardo, however Leo, with his red nose, had been given the name Rudolph by the humans and it stuck with him ever since.

Crazy shit.

Ten Hut!

The reindeer's team leader Blitzen snapped to attention when Nick approached. The rest of the reindeer shuffled themselves into a line, quickly took a knee, then stood upright. They towered above Nick and Carol, each of them standing roughly fifteen feet tall. They were good guys though, and they huddled around the two humans like players in a football match.

"What's the deal Boss? Looks like we have some real problems out there. Is it gonna impact tonight? We are happy to help. Just give me the skinny." Nick liked Blitzen. The reindeer was a no-nonsense, let's just cut the shit kind of animal, and could keep the others in line. The reindeer all had a great sense of humour and were often fucking around with the elves who fortunately didn't mind being the source of a good joke every now and then. In the North Pole, anything to pass the time was welcomed and it was always funny until someone lost an eye and then it was fucking hilarious. Nick thought that felt like a song line, but in the moment wasn't sure.

"Alright guys, thanks for coming here so quickly. It's not looking good. Remember those zombie movies that we watched? Last Halloween?" They nodded and looked back at him. There was a special amphitheater set up for the Elves and reindeer to watch movies together. Being film buffs they would have great discourse on the latest Hollywood releases. Not in a million years would Nick have thought that he would be watching movies with Elves and reindeer, let alone fighting zombies in the wild of the North Pole.

He filled the crew in on what had happened to Tony and the air drop of the Undead. The reindeer had heard the planes overhead. How could they not have? With all those bells, and the ho, ho, ho, it was surprising that the guys at the South Pole hadn't scrambled fighter jets up just to see what the fuck was going on.

Little did Nick know at that time the South Pole had its own problems. In fact, the entire world did.

"Basically guys, what we need you to do is get strapped and get up there. Be mindful of the fact the shield is currently activated. We don't want any flash fried venison for dinner tonight. After all, we've gotta go on a little trip later, all things going well."

Nick didn't want to voice his opinion that he thought Christmas might be canceled this year. He couldn't do that to them. Everyone had worked so hard, and in particular didn't want to let down the millions of children to whom he would have to pretend he had actually eaten their cookies and drank their milk. Everyone was relying on them making this work, and if it meant fighting a horde of zombies to clear the Toy Shop airspace, so be it, that's what they would do. The reindeer talked amongst themselves and took off, heading toward the airstrip, where technicians were waiting with Stinger missiles and launcher harnesses. The Elves quickly put a ladder next to each reindeer and strapped them onto the magnificent creatures' huge shoulders.

Laser pointers were attached to the heads of the reindeer so they could splash their target and the missile would follow where they were looking. It was a surprisingly efficient system, and accounted for the fact that the reindeers were moving, living creatures flying through the air. As long as they were looking at the target, the missile generally hit what it was meant to.

"Okay, so for now, toy manufacture continues. It looks as though we've got enough time to get our quota filled guys." Nick checked his clipboard. "Making sure that everyone in the workshop keeps on going; that is our primary mission. We are going to have to release shields at some stage so I can get out there and do my delivery." Nick looked about seeing his teammates and friends, knowing they were all here for the right reason, and he knew he could rely on every one of them, and they on him.

He looked at Carol and said, "We should be okay sweetheart. Let's just hope that nothing ridiculously unexpected happens."

Big Boy

O ff in the distance, a shambling army of zombies made its way through the forest. It was surprisingly quiet other than a low chant of ho, ho, ho. A few of them had fallen off the Edge of the World, going too close to the edge. A large zombie dressed in a slightly better Santa outfit, made a droning noise that the others seemed to follow. This one appeared to have slightly more intelligence than the rest, and a huge scar over the top of its head from which a light flashed on and off. Wires came out from the back of its skull to a powerpack on its back.

"Ho, ho, ho." The zombies' throats rasped with laughter, moaning softly as they made their way to the twinkling lights down the hill of the Toy Shop. It would still take a while for them to reach their target, which nearly every single one of them was utterly unaware of. A camera took the place of an eyeball in the big zombie's head, and the lens swiveled and buzzed as it tried to get a bearing and focus through the blizzard.

It was as though the creatures of the forest that were normally active were all doing their best to avoid the Undead as they made their way through the woods. Animals streamed through the trees in all directions other than the Edge of the World. For some reason they never seemed to go too close. It was as though they just knew that nothing good waited for them over that precipice. The other creatures of the forest, the ones that were not talked about so much; the genetically altered, misshapen creatures, forgotten by science, and left to fend for themselves, also avoided the oncoming horde by running toward the humming shield. Several were flash fried and evaporated into nothing but dust particles, which the zombies feverishly tried to cram into their mouths as it struck their faces.

A squirrel running ahead of the zombies backed up against one of the shield transmitters and, in its terror, accidentally pissed directly on the box generating the electricity. A crack in the transformer shot a huge amount of electricity into the small, furry creature, scorching it. A stench of cooked squirrel filled the air, and with the surge of power, the transmitter box cracked and fell into pieces.

An Elf team nearby watched in horror as the entire shield protecting the Toy Shop shimmered twice and collapsed.

"Oh, fuck," one said to another "We've got a problem."

Festive Fury

The sound of automatic weapon fire filled the night, echoing all the way back to the Toy Shop. Nick looked up, concerned. Radio chatter came in through the airwaves, informing them that the entire shield had collapsed. The entire workshop was exposed. Christmas might as well go and get truly fucked if these creatures made their way into the hangar and up through to the Toy Shop.

The sleigh was being filled with toys and other equipment right now but wasn't quite ready. Of course the monitoring equipment which Nick was ordered to leave in the atmosphere above enemy countries filled the rest of the sleigh. The technology behind this thing was a miracle, and its capacity to hold millions of items was beyond him, and certainly above his pay grade. Mike the Alien seemed to have an idea of what powered it, however when Nick asked him, he simply shrugged and touched the tip of his non-existent nose with a long gray finger.

Elves ran up and down the sleigh, which was the size of a house, not at all what you would've expected given the prevalence of Christmas movies and Christmas stories. The thing was fucking huge like an armoured personnel carrier and was so heavily reinforced it might as well have been. In the lower depths of the sleigh, five Elves manned mini guns with an undercarriage turret. These were usually covered with cloaking technology in the odd chance that someone would see Nick up in the sky on Christmas Eve, but the sleigh was constantly ready for heavy artillery. The cloaking device on it didn't always work, and more than once the sleigh had come under fire from enemy countries, unable to determine what that flying thing was, or farmers in remote regions taking pot shots at it with their rifles.

The Elves were under strict instructions to not return fire from any non-military source.

In any case, the damn thing was built to take some damage.

Out on the field, the teams fought an increasingly advancing enemy that was not deterred by conventional weaponry. As the bullets whizzed through the night, the jovial moans of the zombies made their way back to the Elves, behind the hastily dug trenches in the snow drift. With the limited amount of time they had, there was no way they could've dug any in the earth, so it was more to give themselves the feeling of cover than anything else. Any true projectile weapon would've punched its way directly through their makeshift shelters inflicting gross injury.

Whomp! The Red Team was concentrating mortar fire on the zombies to the east. Body parts flew everywhere, and still, the zombies kept on coming. The Red Leader looked at his men as they glanced at him for directions. He shrugged, "Just keep on going guys, just keep on going," he said as he tossed a grenade into the thick of the pack just ahead. It lodged itself into the head of a short Santa and detonated. And still, they kept coming. Every now and then a stray bullet would come from the zombie horde as their fingers spasmed and tightened around the triggers of the nearly useless weaponry they were carrying. The advance team that Red Leader had sent forward had yet to report in, and he was worried they'd been overrun.

It seemed that worry was more than justified. Within the forest of red Santa suits, he could see shimmering, green outfits of zombies that had the faces of his friends, their shambling was disconcerted, and they moved with none of the grace that Elves were known for. As the Undead faces coalesced through the snow, Red Leader realized that the horde was way bigger and he would be overrun. There was only one option: to have the best chance of survival, they had to concentrate fire from above, almost directly down on his position, as the horde was close, way too fucking close.

"We need support fire now, we need support fire now! Eastern perimeter is being overrun. Engage Brown Team! Engage, engage! Just be aware we are also going to be in your line of fire. For God's sake, Blitzen, make sure your guys shoot straight! Danger, close, I repeat danger close!"

Red Team heard the radio click clack a couple of times then a confident voice came through "Red Team, this is Brown Team Leader AKA Ya Boi Blitzen. Scrambling now all units, scramble now, eastern wall, danger close, let's get these Undead motherfuckers!"

Oh What Fun It Is To Fly

B ack at the hanger, Blitzen looked at his team. They were fully outfitted with the launchers, and the Elves were placing the last of the missiles on them. Little laser dots pointed as the reindeer moved their heads to and fro talking to each other in hushed tones.

Blitzen moved to the front and said "Alright guys, this is what we've been practicing for. Danger close okay. Red Team have got themselves in a bit of a shit hole and we've gotta help dig it a little bit deeper before they can get out. Enemy forces are there en mass and are currently closing in. If we don't get this right, they're all fucked. As it is, I'm concerned that friendly fire may still impact them. For God's sake, don't get carried away. Keep your lasers pointed at where you want the missile to hit and nowhere else. Until you see a splash you do not move your neck; does everyone understand?"

The reindeer all nodded gravely, they knew the stakes. "And we are ready to rock 'n' roll." Assuming attack formation, the reindeer cantered down the airstrip, and as they ran, whatever black science gave them the ability to get off the ground kicked in, and they flew into the air in triangle formation. There had been no reports of any air resistance, so there was no need to fly covertly. As he took off, Blitzen rubbed his chin against the sprig of mistletoe that one of the Elves had hung around his neck for luck. *We are going to need it*, he thought, and they lifted up into the clouds, preparing to dive down on the eastern border.

R.U.D.Y

N ick and Carol heard the chatter of combat and were getting situation reports from the other leaders. The situation looked as grim as in the east, even though the Elves were holding their own. Currently, the zombie onslaught was taking its toll on all fronts. This was the problem with fighting the Undead; unless you took care of your own once they were attacked, they instantly became the enemy within thirty seconds to a minute. That was intel that they did not have access to prior to this; just how quickly the infection spread from the dead to the living.

Nick wracked his brains trying to find how they could possibly get an edge in the battle. At this rate Christmas was done and dusted, and children all over the world would be missing out. Even worse, if kids doubted the story of Christmas and Santa Claus, The Agency may need to close the Toy Shop, which presented a problem for everyone involved. Without the Toy Shop and its defense systems in place, all of the nukes in the silo underneath the Base would be exposed for the entire world to know about. The Toy Shop needed to exist for more than spreading joy. The security of the entire free world, depending on which side you were on, relied on it.

Carol interrupted his thoughts. She was holding a brightly painted wooden box with a glass front. Inside it was a huge plastic candy cane. The box had a simple sticker on the front that read Break In Case of Emergency Only.

"Is that the cane from behind my desk?" Nick asked. Carol nodded. "Yes love it is, and I think considering how fucked the situation is, it might be time to break it." She handed Nick a small hammer commonly used in the workshop to make wooden ducks.

"Okay let's do this," Nick said, tapping the hammer against the glass, which shattered almost immediately.

"Mind your hands sweetheart." Carol pulled out the cane and handed it to Nick. Once he unscrewed the handle there was a tube containing a scroll with hand lettered instructions. As he read through them, his brow furrowed and finally Carol said, "What does it say?"

Nick looked up at her and said, "It says we have to go down to the very bottom of the Base. It says something about a weapon down there, classified only by an acronym: R.U.D.Y."

Elf Carnage

B ack into the corridor they went and carefully opened the sealed door. It wasn't even locked, which Nick thought was kinda weird, but didn't have time to really reflect on it. At the end of a short passageway there was a lift that went down at least 50 floors underground and eventually the lift doors opened up into a small foyer that was decked out like a reasonably priced hotel. Making their way past a concierge desk which was abandoned, even though they rang the bell twice with confusion, they went down a small hall that only contained one door.

"Curiouser and Curiouser" said Carol.

On the door was a brass plaque embossed with the letters. RUDY. Nick knocked, and a pleasant voice called out, "Please come in. Mind to take your boots off if you would be so kind."

Inside the room which was filled with mahogany and fur was a large bed with a bearskin rug in front of it. The head of the bear was not a real one, but a fake fur rug with a teddy bear head at the end. There was a television with the volume muted showing scenes from the battle via the multiple body cams that were out there on the field. A large wing chair contained a body watching the television as a plume of smoke occasionally rose from the chair, and a hand reached out to grasp a crystal tumbler of whiskey on ice.

"Hello?", Nick called out slowly and the chair turned around and the occupant faced them. It was an Elf, dressed in a smoking jacket, wearing slippers, gold rimmed spectacles and an expensive watch. A cravat adorned his neck and his gray hair was brushed back stylishly as he took a puff from a long handled pipe. Despite the hair, it was nearly impossible to figure out his age. Some Elves were just born with gray hair and his face was almost wrinkle free. The tobacco smoke was rich and filled with hints of rum and wood. The Elf took another puff, considered them both for a moment, and then said in a very rich melodic voice.

"Well, since you're here, I'm guessing you broke the candy cane. My name is Rudy, how may I be of service."

"Hi there Rudy", Carol said. "I'm Carol."

Rudy chuckled. "We can dispense with the pleasantries dear, I know who you both are. Good job so far. Don't blame yourself for what's going on now, I've been watching the battle since the beginning, and I agree it's probably time for me to get involved, though I was never designed to take on the Undead."

"What do you mean designed?" Nick asked.

Rudy looked him in the eye, taking Nick's measure. "Quite frankly old chap, I'm a killing machine. One of your last lines of defense, when, as they say, the shit goes down. I'm the one that you get on board when there are no other options."

"Why is that?" Nick asked. "I'm really sorry Rudy. I'm sure that you're a good guy, but I can't see anything here that would change the course of battle, especially against these enemies." He looked around the room, waiting to see some secret panel open up and a lot of weapons expose themselves. *Maybe remote access to the nukes?* Yeah no idea, but they needed to hurry up. Time was of the essence both for Christmas and for the lives of all the Elves out there on the field.

"Fair point Nick. It may not be obvious to you, but trust me, I am more than capable of taking on this enemy." Rudy took another puff of his pipe and let out the smoke slowly in lazy concentric rings.

Then he looked Nick square in the eye and said, "I have rabies."

An Unexpected Advantage

Nick took a step back. "What the fuck?" he said. "Are you fucking kidding me? Is this some sort of joke?"

"Not at all," Rudy answered. "See under my cravat." He pulled it aside to reveal a collar. "This is an inhibitor collar designed by the Agency to keep my more.... let's say crazy tendencies in check, but I can tell you right now; take this collar off and I'm one fully cooked unit. I'd rip you apart before you knew I'd done it. I'd rip out your eyeballs, feed them to Carol, then slit her throat before your sight had the chance to tell your brain that you could no longer see. I'd dismember her and smack you in the head with the bloody part of a stump, then make you vomit by sticking the fingers of her dead hand down your throat. Then I'd disembowel you and cut open the contents of your stomach, and feed the non-digested ones to Carol before you bled out, then I'd-"

"Enough! I get the fucking point, you've got rabies," Nick said. "Exactly," Rudy said, settling back down on the chair. "So should we get down to business and fuck some shit up?" Nick looked at Carol, a question in his eyes. *What the hell was this?* She shrugged. What else were they going to do at this point? Rudy must've been down here for a reason. He seemed quietly confident and very unhinged. She kind of liked the Elf and wished that they had got the chance to meet him under different circumstances. Of course, all of those circumstances involved him still having that inhibitor collar on.

"Come on Rudy," she said. "Let's go up and quickly meet the team." They made their way to the elevator and rode to the surface.

Flying Fur

B rown Team began its first bombing run. Blitzen adjusted his headset. The reindeer didn't really need the headsets; they could communicate telepathically. Unfortunately, the two humans on the ground and the Elves didn't have that luxury. They needed to hear all the stuff that he was telling his team, so they could coordinate these attacks better. "Hi guys, almost there. Get ready."

Even up in the sky he could hear the slight hum as the missile launchers were activated by the reindeer shrugging their shoulders forward. He felt adrenaline coursing through his body and tried to shrug it off. You needed a clear head, especially as they were going to be firing down near the Elves. From the ground, he could hear Nick and Carol talking to other color leaders through the headsets. Something about a weapon called Rudy. He had no idea what they were talking about. For a brief moment he thought they were talking about Rudolph, though that couldn't be the case. Rudolph was a stickler when it came to his name. Well, his fake name anyhow, and would only answer to Rudolph.

"Begin downward assault."

As one, the reindeer spread apart to give each other room to fire, and dove down towards the zombie horde. They could see the Elves hunkered behind snow hills, and knew that defense was useless against the weapons that they were about to fire. Accuracy was key in achieving the objective.

As they dived down, the zombies came into view. "Fire. Fire. Fire." Blitzen barked into his headset. Missiles left launchers as the reindeer concentrated their view into the main mass of the Undead. "Stay together, stay together," Blitzen said. They had to complete this pass first in order to give the missiles time to hit the ground. Keeping together was key in ensuring this happened without casualties to themselves.

"I can get another round in Boss," he heard Dasher call out to him telepathically.

"No son, we don't have time. Just wait for the second pass." Blitzen hoped that for once the enthusiastic reindeer would simply do as he was told.

"I can do it. I'm sure I can make it!"

"You won't have time to pull up. Forget that, that's a direct order. We can fire again on the next pass. Don't you dare fucking go ahead on us, stay with the group!"

It was too late. Dasher, as always, the fastest of the group, thought he could make it out of the bombing dive quickly enough to get in another shot, and as he arched his back to try to get airborne again, he clipped the top of a tree and went tumbling into the snow. The second missile and shoulder harness fired harmlessly into a snowdrift, the splash damage did lift a couple of zombies up into the air, but otherwise did not really affect anything. It certainly didn't slow down the mob that descended upon the impetuous reindeer, their teeth closing in on his fur with a relentless ferocity that left the whole group cold. He could hear the yelling of the other reindeer in his head; they wanted to go down there and save their brother. He ordered them all to stop, and thank God they all listened. There was no way he could be saved at this point. There were just too many of them on the ground. Dasher thrashed about as the teeth closed in on his flesh, the zombies even tried to bite through the metal of his armaments, breaking their teeth and jaws, and still not caring. He felt their claws raking through his flesh as he kicked out and smashed skulls as best he could, but it was too late.

Too many bites, too much of their shitty saliva in his system already. The wounds felt like they were immediately infected; a sickly warmth started to go through him like a super flu or a virus that was making his body burn up. He heard the cries of the other reindeer in his head and the horror they felt for him. It was too late, too late for anything but for him to say "I love you guys, I'm really sorry. Don't come down here. I love you love y...."

His body thrashed and twitched a couple more times then lay still. No longer alive, the zombies lost interest in him and slowly crawled back to their feet. Continuing toward the Toy Shop, the distance was closing rapidly. Circling back around, Blitzen saw his brother laying still and spoke into his headset:

"Big Poppa, this is Brown Leader. First strike unsuccessful. I repeat, first strike unsuccessful, and we've lost one. Dasher is gone."

Back at the Base, the Elves gathered around Rudy. Most of them were aware of his existence, though they had thought it was an urban legend; a rabid Elf kept at the bottom of the Toy Shop at the North Pole? That sounded like something out of a stupid short story, written by an unknown author. Yet here he was, as he demonstrated some of his fighting techniques on a hastily set up series of mats on the floor.

As he quickly went through different fighting styles that they might adopt, the Elves found it hard to keep up. He moved with a speed that was beyond theirs and was all claws and teeth. Over the years, Elves had come to rely a lot more on basic hand-to-hand combat using weapons, this primal style of fighting was something that they were not accustomed to, and it was not working. They simply could not keep up with Rudy.

Eventually the rabid Elf stopped what he was doing and said to Nick, "This isn't working. I work alone or not at all. Just let me do what I do best. It sounds as though we are not doing so well out there, so it's probably a good idea for me to get going."

Over the radio, they heard Blitzen announce that Dasher had fallen. A sorrowful sound made its way throughout the building. The reindeer were all adored by the Elves. In fact, they were loved by everyone, even Mike the Alien, and to hear that one of them had fallen was heartbreaking.

Nick wiped away a tear and thumbed the button on his radio. "Ground Leader. This is Big Poppa. I am so fucking sorry. And I'm sorry to say, but I need you to stay focused. We need that second run regardless of its outcome. At the very least, it will be a good distraction. Split up your team two per squad and go to every front using your last missiles on the biggest mass. Hopefully we can take some of these fuckers out and at least slow them up. Red Team, Blue Team, Green Team and Yellow Team are doing their best, but they are being overrun. We need to buy them enough time to fill the sleigh so we can go wheels up ASAP."

Nick started to turn off the radio and had an idea. He clicked the button back down. "Brown Leader? This is Big Poppa. Send Little Beacon back to Base, I have a job for him."

He turned around and looked at Rudy. "Let's get you outside and get you airborne. Rudolph is on his way."

Revenge with a Dash of Red

T he Santa zombies had almost made their way to the outer buildings of the Toy Shop and their "Ho, ho, ho" chants echoed amongst the shadows as their bodies cast ghastly silhouettes around the entire Base. Mixed in with all this were the brave Elven team leaders, and their soldiers attempting to stave off the hordes. They made little to no impact as these things kept on going, and it was nearly impossible in the dark to squeeze off good headshots with every single round fired. These things were bullet sponges, and even the best placed headshots wouldn't always achieve the job.

With a heavy thud, Rudolph hit the tarmac and came skittering to a stop in front of Nick and Carol. "Boss," he said. From behind them Rudy stepped out. He was dressed in green combat fatigues, and had a bondola of grenades slung over his shoulders. Wickedly sharp hunting knives were stuck into belts over his body, along with two very long and tapered picks. "Permission to get on board," Rudy said. Rudolph lowered himself down and allowed the rabid Elf to hop onto his back. Rudy's cravat flowed in the breeze as Nick wished him all the best.

"Rest assured," Rudy said. "I'll do my best."

As Nick talked to Rudy, Carol reached up and wrapped her arms around Rudolph's neck. He nuzzled his face into her nape, as she cradled him and gave him a kiss. She stroked his snout for a brief moment, and gave him a nod. He looked at her gravely and gave a short shake of his massive head. His nose began to pulse as he prepared himself for flight mode. She stepped back to give him room for takeoff. With Rudy on his back, Rudolph wheeled about and started to run back down the runway. He achieved lift off, curious about the cargo he carried. He said as much, and Rudy gave an abrupt laugh and held onto the fur of Rudolph's neck a little bit tighter, leaning forward against the howling wind. He whispered with a tone that made Rudolph shiver. "I'm your secret weapon, old chap. I've got rabies."

They flew into the night air and headed east. Absently, Rudy scratched behind Rudolph's ears. The reindeer arched his head back, taking care to not gouge out Rudy's eyes with antlers.

"Oh, my god! That feels so good!" Rudolph exclaimed as his nose blinked on and off in flight mode. "Well, there's plenty more where that came from, old boy," Rudy said, as he kept his hand around his pipe and lit it. Rudolph saw the glow from the pipe and snickered.

"I'm very sorry, sir, but this is a non-smoking flight." Rudy smiled as he took a puff, and with the other hand continued to scratch Rudolph around his ears and chin.

"It's quite alright my boy. I won't tell them if you don't. Now let's get cracking." He felt at the collar underneath his cravat.

"It's nearly time to cut loose, boy."

Santa's Workshop of Horrors

C arol shook her head. So many gifts left to wrap at the front part of the Toy Shop. The Elves were still in full production mode, despite the fact that a zombie war was taking place directly out the front of their doorstep. This was Christmas Eve, and they didn't have the luxury of halting production, despite the fact that there was still a very good chance of being eradicated before the night was through. The sleigh was overflowing with gifts and things to delight. In the hidden compartments, top secret monitoring devices were ready to be launched. The miniguns were loaded, and the Elves were onboard. They may have to run and gun to leave, and be ready for anything.

"At the moment guys, things aren't looking great," Nick said. "We have teams surrounding the Base but they are falling fast. I'm really sorry, I feel like I've let you down, but we never anticipated anything like this. The whole thing feels like something out of a Z grade horror movie. Be that as it may, the zombies are still outside and we are doing our best to make sure it stays that way, but you need to do your best now more than ever to make sure that fucking sleigh is filled with toys because if this is going to be the last Christmas ever, we're going to do it right! Okay?"

The Elves cheered and got back to work. Soldiers gripped their rifles as they guarded the two entryways to the Toy Shop.

"Any news on Rudy, Nick?" Carol asked as they left the Toy Shop. They heard the doors being bolted behind them, and the sound of Christmas music coming back over the speakers. It wasn't as though they were hiding anything from those inside; they were fully aware of the risks, but there was no point in distracting them from their more important task as far as both Nick and Carol were concerned. Outside might be madness and mayhem, but inside the workshop it should be nothing but bustle, bustle, bustle.

"Rudolph's getting him out to the eastern perimeter," Nick said. "I've half a mind to head out there myself. It doesn't feel right sending all the guys out there, and I'm just kicking back here telling them what to do."

Carol shook her head and said, "Well honey, unfortunately that's just the way it is at the end of the day. To the rest of the world *you* are Santa Claus, and more to the point we do have a mission to uphold, and the sleigh is genetically coded to only work for you." It had always been failsafe of The Agency to build top level security into every incarnation of the sleigh as technology changed and improved. In the early days anyone could jump in and take it for a spin, but after that disaster in 1869, they had decided that only one person should be the sole driver of what was arguably the world's most advanced combat system. Nick nodded. She was always right, that's why he loved her so much. He just didn't like being the person who sent people out to possibly die. In fact, casualties were coming back right now, and some of the Elves were spending as many bullets making sure their friends stayed dead, as opposed to taking out the actual zombies themselves.

"Alright love, please understand it just doesn't sit right with me, but I get what you're saying. Let's hope we get to do the delivery at all." He shook his head.

Knock Knock? Who's there? We Are!

As the department store Santas stumbled and made their way across the frozen North Pole Base, they eventually came upon the outer perimeter of the Toy Shop itself. Lifeless limbs scrabbled intently at a door that would not open, and gradually the Santas piled up and over the top of each other in a ghastly red and white mountain that eventually was too heavy for the door itself which splintered. It was just an access door that the apprentice chefs took the rubbish out after a meal to the bins that waited, but the combined weight of over fifty zombies caved it in.

At first, there was a light crack across the surface that eventually a hand punched through to the other side of the door. It looked like something was trying to burrow its way through. Eventually more chunks of the door were thrown to the side, and the first zombie face appeared, glancing about aimlessly as its white bloodsoaked beard poked through the crack like a cotton bud. Then the door gave way and collapsed in, falling straight down, crushing an Elf under it as bodies tumbled. One of the Santas, sensing living flesh below the door, started trying to poke its lower jaw and tongue through the gap, ripping itself apart with the long splinters that became embedded in its mouth. The Elf, a young man only a couple of hundred years old, was crushed under the weight and asphyxiated. The zombies, no longer sensing life, ignored the corpse below them and started to move down the hallway to the kitchen, drawn to the clatter of pots and pans. They entered the Toy Shop dining area unnoticed over the din of the kitchen.

Meanwhile, back up on an icy hill, the lead zombie stood still, as its controller surveyed the battlefield. They were getting closer to what they were truly there for... They were getting closer to the nukes.

Jetset

"So, what's the deal?" Rudolph asked Rudy as they prepared to descend from the clouds. Rudy had been limbering up on the saddle, moving about and stretching. He could feel his battle ferocity intensifying as he saw the carnage below. It was only a matter of time before he'd be able to slip the inhibitor collar off his neck. Once that was done, *Rudolph needed to get the hell out of there*, he thought to himself. Generally, Rudy was able to control himself despite the rabies and could discern friend from foe, but he would not forgive himself if he accidentally jumped on, or even worse, killed someone he considered a friend.

The Elf Team Leaders had all been given inhibitor collars to try and capture Rudy after the fight, but it would be a matter of getting them onto his neck when he was in full battle mode, and that in and of itself would prove to be a heck of a problem.

"Well old chap, it's simple." Rudy reached up, and grasped the release mechanism on the collar. "At the right moment, I'm gonna jump off your back, yes from a great height, and I'm going to plunge down into the thick of things and fuck shit up to put it colloquially. At some point one poor bugger is going to have to try to put a collar back on me, and there's a good chance I might resist, especially if I'm overcome with bloodlust." He said all this so matter-of-factly that Rudolph shivered. Rudy felt the movement and added, "It should be okay old boy, it should be okay. In any case, if we see our way clear, I'd really like to continue this conversation over a nice cognac if that would suit you?" The two had had quite the chat en route and the feeling was mutual. As they lowered, the battleground came clear into focus and Rudy noticed the larger zombie standing up at the back of the battlefield.

"See that one back there?" He pointed past Rudolph's nose. "That one up there I think is the problem. I think I need to work my way up to him. If you wouldn't mind clearing an opening for me, that would be much appreciated." He patted one of the missiles loaded onto Rudolph's shoulders. Rudolph nodded. "No problem, can do. You might actually want to take what's on my nose. It might come in handy. I think you're going to need it more than I will. Can you see it?" He paused, and sensed Rudy's confusion.

"Ha! Ha! Honestly, can't you see it? Or do you think that my nose really is a bulbous red light? That's just something the kids sing. Carol gave me a parting gift. That thing on my nose is not just a pretty light. It's a thermal detonator."

Rudy leaned past Rudolph's head and unsnapped the clasps holding the detonator to the reindeer's nose. "I'll take that old boy, and be most obliged in the taking. That would've been a right bugger to remove yourself let alone throw. You know… opposable thumbs and all that."

Rudolph slowed his flight just a little bit so that he could turn his head safely. He looked Rudy in the eye and said, "That detonator was a one-way trip. There is no way in Hell I could remove it. And before you say anything, I told Carol to put it there after Dasher…" He took a deep, shattering breath, and continued, "After Dasher was torn apart, I just wanted to take out as many as I possibly could, even if it meant taking myself out in the process. But I honestly think you might have a chance of doing a lot more good with it than I would simply flying it into a group of them…"

Rudy handled the detonator gingerly, aware of its immense explosive power. He knew that once the collar was off, he really wouldn't care how big a BOOM it would make. He just hoped that he had enough of his wits about him to get clear of its blast radius.

"Thanks chap. Okay, I think it's time for us to part ways, for the time being at least." He unhooked his feet from the stirrups, and crouched atop Rudolph's saddle. The wind made it hard to stand there and he felt himself wobble about.

"As soon as I feel you jump, I'm going to fire both missiles ahead of you," Rudolph said. "They'll easily beat you to the ground and won't pose a problem, but hopefully it'll clear enough of a path to give you a head start." The reindeer felt a final firm scratch behind both of his ears, and then pressure on his back as Rudy left. Rudolph focused on the ground, aiming straight at a large pack of zombies below. Their creepy "Ho. Ho. Ho." noise rising up from the ground.

"Ho, ho, ho, yourself, motherfuckers!" He shrugged his shoulders and the missiles leapt from the shoulder launchers. Rudolph made sure he kept the laser pointing at the pack even as he circled above the battlefield, the red dot remaining steady as he saw a green flash of color following the projectiles. *Go get them you little bastard,* he thought to himself as the missiles hit the ground, scattering limbs, blood and guts everywhere with a fireball pluming upward, engulfing Rudy. *Go get them you magnificent bastard.*

He did one final circle, but couldn't see anything through the smoke and fire. Then out of the corner of his eye, he saw something silver twinkling as it descended to earth. Rudy's inhibitor collar, no longer around the neck of its owner. He almost pitied the zombies knowing what was headed their way, then he flew back to join his squadron for more ammunition.

Toy Shop Slaughterhouse

Outside the Toy Shop, the battle raged unabatedly. Automatic weapon fire and explosions filled the night air with screams, moans, and ho, ho, ho's. Body parts were scattered all over the once pristine Base and when the Elves ran out of bullets, arms and legs were used as bludgeoning tools. The battle was rapidly being lost and the Elves knew it, yet they still fought on, determined to preserve Christmas at all costs. Overhead, the reindeer were up to their third attack run, but knew there was no point in firing any more as the missiles would have splashed directly into the Toy Shop on top of both zombies and Elves, and there would have been more friendly fire than enemy fire. Which indirectly would've made it an unfriendly, friendly fire.

Inside, the Elves protecting the Toy Shop never really stood a chance. The zombies made their way through the bolted doors, breaking them through sheer force of numbers, and then overwhelming the guards and their rifles.

The sounds of gunfire and bullets zipping through the air brought toy production to a standstill. One of the supervisors switched off the loudspeakers playing carols, and the music died off, leaving nothing but the sound of heavy panting and department store Santa zombies moaning "Ho. Ho. Ho." Blood and guts splattered the doorways of the Toy Shop, where zombies frantically licked the gory debris off any surface they could find whilst it was still warm. Then they got to their feet and shambled forward only to find heavily armed Elves ready to throw down.

Firecrackers whistled their way through the confined space. Bottle rockets were shot with unerring precision into the eye sockets of zombies, their heads exploding under the pressure. One Santa twisted around in a comical pirouette, whilst fireworks detonated throughout its body. An Elf unloaded a full tray of marbles across the floor, causing the Undead to slip and slide. It would've been funny, if not for the fact that failure would've meant becoming the creature's next meal. Inside the sleigh, the gunners frantically warmed up the chainguns. Last resort here; there was no way they wanted to open fire inside the Toy Shop. One of the elves slipped on the marbles, and slid under the massive shuffling feet, their owners descending upon her. Hideous screams rose as she was eaten, chilling the blood of even the most impassioned fighters and made worse by the fact that about forty seconds later, she rose as one of the Undead. Her torn apart face twitched horrifically as her glazed-over eyes locked on her friends and family. But no longer as people she cared about. They were now about to be her first meal.

All of a sudden it dawned on Jerry, one of the supervisors at the Toy Shop, that there was a peculiar pattern to the movements of the zombie horde.

"Everyone listen!" he yelled above the din of combat, the Elves struggling to hear him. "We have a better chance if we can get all these things outside!" he said. "They're after us, not the sleigh." Zombie eyes locked on to him as the source of the most commotion and started shambling in Jerry's direction as he slowly backed up and moved toward the door.

Joey looked up from where he was gouging out the eyes of a department store Santa zombie with a spring toy. It wobbled backward and forward as he screwed it through the orbital socket, eventually puncturing the brain and halting all function. "No shit, Jerry. They're fucking zombies, but you do have a point. Hey! Ho! Let's go!"

Gradually the Elves were able to entice the zombies to follow them out of the Toy Shop, the automatic guns on the sleigh slowly lowered into the resting position. Though the zombies were super keen to eat anything with a heartbeat, magical or otherwise, they appeared to be attracted to that which was making the most noise. Using whatever weapons were closest at hand, and in this case mainly toys, the Elves fended off the attack as they made their way from the Toy Shop.

"The warning labels are gonna have to be changed on these!" Cyndi grunted as she grabbed a popular brand of doll, and using a hammer from a superhero playset, thwacked its feet through the eye sockets of yet another zombie, the sound of plastic on plastic barely audible above the zombies, who had not ceased "Ho, Ho, Ho'ing" the entire time. Eventually, the entire rotting, bloody mess of zombies and Elves made its way back up the long corridor leading outside.

Stop, Drop, and Roll

Whomp! Rudy hit the ground. Hard. He breathed heavily, and realized that he was stuck in the snow. He also realized that he had a lot more control over his faculties than he thought he would have, feeling the rabies burning through his blood, tightening his muscles. He ran his fingers over his abdominal area, and felt the hard knots of muscle in his stomach. *You've still got it old boy,* Rudy thought to himself as he smiled, and felt his sharp canines pushing into his bottom lip. He wiped his mouth with the back of his hand, and saw foam and flecks of blood on it. The smell was intoxicating and he inhaled again and licked the mess off his hand.

"Owoooooooooooooooo!" he howled into the night, the commotion bringing the closest of the department store Santas whirling about to face him. One was so rotten that as it twisted, its leg literally sheared from its hip, causing it to tumble to the ground. The others however, were still mobile and started clambering toward him. "Bring it on bitches!" Rudy used his hands to pull his own feet out of the snow. The cold was invigorating, and he realized he'd been cooped up, smoking his pipe, wearing a robe and slippers for far too long.

This was what he was made for; this is what he loved. Running toward the oncoming Undead he leaped into the air with the grace of a ballerina, and did a forward somersault that an Olympic gymnast would've been proud of, bringing his knees up to his chest as he did so. The rabid Elf felt the wind rushing through his hair, stinging his eyes. As he descended after what felt like an eternity, he extended his legs out fully with the heels of his boots foremost to the ground. The zombie stuck in the snow didn't stand a chance, yet its Undead eyes did not even widen in surprise as Rudy's boots caved its face in, destroying its entire head.

"Ha ha ha ha! Jingle Bell, Jingle Bell, Jingle Bell Rock, I'll cave in your head then I'll kick you in the-"

He stopped mid song, just in time for the comedic effect to have kicked in, and knew the reader would finish that line he was singing with what was no doubt a swear word.

Rudy reached behind his back and pulled out two ice picks and twirled them about his fingers like a drummer at a rock concert. They flashed in the light, sending sparkles of silver into the eyes of the nearest zombie, temporarily blinding it. Rudy somersaulted this time on the ground and jumped up high in the air, driving the ice picks down as he did so into the top of the Santa's head. The baubles and ornamentation on its hat slowed down the skull puncture a fraction more than what Rudy would've liked, giving it the opportunity to claw blindly at him in its attempt to feed.

He felt a strong wiry hand grip his pants as it started to tear through them. "Not without buying me dinner, Romeo!" He smacked the second pick down hard and heard a satisfying crunch as the Santa slumped in the snow, releasing its clutch on his leg. He moved forward without giving it a second look and tried to locate the third Santa. There it was, hunkered down, nibbling on a baby rabbit it had stumbled upon. Ripping the small creature's head clear off its body, the zombie got to its feet with the rabbit head dangling by its ears from its mouth. It was still trying to rasp out a 'Ho, Ho, Ho', but all that did was make it look as though the rabbit was trying to talk to Rudy.

He laughed and tried to stop himself. That wasn't funny, baby rabbits being eaten wasn't funny. But a baby rabbit's head talking to him from the zombies mouth... his giggles burst into laughter, and he was keenly aware that no one else was there who would've appreciated this joke. He knew it was the rabies, but at this point he didn't care. He had to keep reminding himself to not get any blood into his mouth that was not his own. His body shook as a hot flash went through him, and he felt the perspiration break out on his head. Yet, for some reason, he could still control the majority of his thoughts and movement; they were just exaggerated by the virus.

He looked ahead and saw the hordes descending toward him on a hill. The giant Santa was barely visible. It must've been the one he saw earlier. *So, you're the daddy eh? Well, lucky for you it's Father's Day and I've got a present for you in my pants!* He patted the thermal detonator zipped into his pocket and moved towards the horde. It was going to be quite a fight.

Zombie Reindeer Rampage: A Bloody Ballet

The reindeer were exhausted. Their fur was damp with both sweat and rain. Their hooves were awash with blood and brains from various dive bombing parties where they kicked in the heads of the zombies that made their way toward the Toy Shop. Despite their best efforts, they had watched as the zombies broke into the Base, powerless to do anything about it. There were just too many.

Blitzen radioed, "Nick! Nick! Nick! I hope everything is going okay on your end. Just a heads up we've lost control of the pack inside the Base. Repeat, they are inside the Base. All Elves should be on high alert. Those fuckers are headed to the Toy Shop if they are not in there already!" He whirled about, leaning heavily onto his front legs bucking and kicking wildly, caving in the head and chest of a female department store Santa. He wondered about it for a second as he had never seen one of those. It was a changing world that's for sure.

The zombie made a husky, ho, ho, ho sound from its throat, then died, falling to the ground in front of its fellow Santas, briefly slowing their advance. He looked up at the rest of Brown Team who all looked as exhausted as he was. It was kind of weird; they flew the entire world in just one night, and they spent the entire year training for that, but several hours of battle was taking its toll, not to mention quite literally their lives.

Poor Dasher, he thought to himself. The reindeer had been a sweet kid and would be missed. At the rate they were going, the reindeer would be pinned in if they didn't get moving. Close quarters combat was one thing, but with the amount of zombies that were there, and the fact that they were fighting under a rooftop, things were not going to go well if he didn't get his team out fast.

"Abort! Abort! Back to HQ," Blitzen yelled out loud and telepathically. Immediately the entire team levitated as one and made their way back to the stables with several zombies grasping their legs and clawing at them as they dangled in midair. Blitzen made his way back to Prancer, who was being weighed down by the sheer amount of Undead, holding on as he tried to follow the team. The zombie's claws had made a mess of Prancer's fur, and the reindeer looked positively panicked. That was the last thing the team needed flying in close quarters formation; one of them losing the plot.

"You're okay!" Blitzen pushed the thought directly at Prancer. The reindeer heard the powerful communication and turned to look at his leader. Blitzen said, "Don't forget, blood and spit are the killers; their fingers won't do that to you. You're okay, just help me kick these fuckers off you." Prancer shook his legs violently, literally scraping zombies against each other in an attempt to dislodge them. Blitzer aimed carefully in midair, and booted as hard as he could, taking care not to kick his teammate in the legs, which would've instantly broken them. Eventually, the Undead were all cleared, and they were able to make their way back to Base.

"We'll get you patched up quickly. Grab a bite to eat and get back out there." Prancer nodded, and they descended gradually as the stables came into view. Blitzen's eyes widened as he saw the zombies had also made their way into Brown Team HQ. *This is some bullshit,* he thought to himself. He could see through the windows as the entire area was packed, and there was no way they were going to ever get these shit heels out of there without really risking harm to themselves.

"Stay back, stay back. Brown Team, stay back," he commanded, and the reindeer stopped, hovering in the air. He hoped that the Elves had not gone into the stables after them, as at this point, he just knew that the stables were lost. He also knew that he could not risk the zombies or anyone else for that matter getting their hands on some of the technology that was being developed there.

Hark! The Machete Blade Sings!

Nick whirled around, his red robes flying about, his machete gleaming, slicked with blood. Little parts of the blade were serrated and broken from caving in skulls. Next to him, he heard Carol thrusting a javelin she had taken from the Toy Shop earlier. Despite the fact it had a point on both ends, she still had to exert quite an amount of force in order to do damage and he could tell she was tiring. It was a weird sensation fighting side-by-side like this; both terrifying and exciting. They had not had to do anything like this since that one operation that went bad in the Middle East where, running out of ammo, they had to resort to very unconventional weaponry in order to escape.

His communication module crackled, and he heard Blitzen announce that the Toy Shop was being invaded. He hesitated for a moment, wondering if he needed to make his way back there or if they should still make their way back up to the surface. He knew the sleigh was heavily fortified and decided the surface would be the best bet. The Elves formed a protective ring around Nick and Carol with the occasional zombie slipping through. So far, he had not lost too many of his team, and they had kept their cool for the most part.

The sounds of combat echoed up and down the hallway, and eventually they could see at the end of the corridor, the light of the night sky casting its gentle light downward. It was tough going, the corridor inclining steeply towards the end, slick with the blood and brains of both Elves and zombies. On more than one occasion, someone would slip and fall in the stew and have to rapidly be pulled to their feet before they were overwhelmed. The radio vibrated and he listened intently just in time to hear Blitzen say the code word Scorched Earth.

Holy shit! He knew what that meant. The stables had been overrun, and even he knew there were things in there that should never fall into the hands of anyone outside the Agency. Fuck the nukes under the Toy Shop, they paled by comparison with what those damn reindeer were making in the stables. Oh well, it could all be rebuilt. Or could it? *Also, how the hell did they make anything out there without hands?*

"Fire! Fire! Fire!" The explosion threw them all to the ground as shockwaves reverberated throughout the Toy Shop as Blitzen flicked the switch. It blew up the high yield explosives that were built into every supporting wall of the stable complex. Such was the force of the explosion that the reindeers themselves were pushed back through the air in which they hovered, falling to their sides mid flight, sending them crashing to the Earth below. For the longest time, it was thought that the reindeer could actually sleep in the air, and it was disproven after a drunken night when one of them, Blitzen couldn't remember who now, thought that they would take a nap mid-flight to the laughter of everyone else.

The sight of a reindeer plummeting to earth however, quickly sobered them up and two of the guys had managed to quickly wake the slumbering idiot before he splattered all over the deck. Actually, Blitzen realized with a tinge of sadness it was Dasher.

Boom, Shake the Room

J ust moments before the explosions ripped the stables apart, the whole compound was silent with the sounds of distant combat, barely audible. There was an overwhelming crashing sound, and one of the entrances was breached by a group of zombies wired up similarly to the large Santa who was controlling the whole shindig. Streams of data flowed through their receptors into what was left of their brains.

This was the reason for the whole attack; to get to the R&D section of the stables. Getting to the nukes would've been a bonus, but the stables were the reason for the air drop. As the doors opened, the zombie operator could just see into the darkness through the optical receptors of the various units he was controlling, then all went dark as the reindeer defense measures kicked in and scrambled all communications, rendering them ineffective to the point of useless. Unguided, the zombies made their way into the stables and blundered about aimlessly, the smell of the reindeer was old now, as they had been in the air battling for quite some time, and without a smell of fresh meat, zombies were next to useless as an effective fighting force.

Blitzen's voice came over the speakers inside the stables. The zombies made their way to the sound source.

'Ho. Ho. Ho. Boom! Dickheads. This is for Dasher."

Chunks of rotten meat flew through the air, still encased in Santa costumes. Fragments of the complex splashed with red blood and gore stood out against the stark white of the snow of the North Pole. In the distance the lead Santa zombie could see the abject failure of his strike team. Not that he personally cared; he had been dead for quite some time, but the operator controlling him did. Within a darkened room on the other side of the world, he struck his fist down on the desk, causing the Santa zombie to mimic his actions, punching down hard, causing the creature below him to grunt, and wobble on its feet.

Glancing down, the big Santa saw the shaggy fur, and a twisted smile crossed its ruined face. The operator caused the animated corpse to kick what was left of Dasher in the ribs, and the zombie reindeer slowly lifted into the air, carrying the massive Santa on its back.

Maybe, the operator thought, *it was beginning to look alot like Christmas* after all.

The Trooper

R udy plowed through the zombie horde, leaving a trail of permanently dead behind him. Blood and guts filled the landscape and the rabid Elf surged toward the massive Santa on the hill. As he sliced and diced his way through grasping, clawed hands and gnashing teeth, he had to keep reminding himself that these were imposters in cheap costumes, not the real deal. Over the years with The Agency, Rudy had gotten to know, and like the Agents that they had sent, but with the exception of that one night a year with a sortie flown over the world, the Agents never referred to themselves as Santa and Mrs Claus. Not that it was forbidden by any paragraph in the manual that The Agency provided, it just seemed wrong.

Rudy had known the first Santa. Not just known of him, but was friends with him when he first started The Agency's outpost here after discovering the North Pole, and of course, its peculiar inhabitants. Curiosity attracted the Elf to the location, as it had many of his brothers and sisters. They had for years been involved in the affairs of humanity behind the scenes, and this was too good an opportunity to be passed up.

It has been a weird time; a time of new beginnings at the Toy Shop. It had quickly been built up, as had the mythology of Christmas. It was funny how quickly both adults and children gravitated towards this story; a fat man in a red suit dumping gifts off a sleigh propelled by flying reindeer? Humans would believe anything. Rudy laughed to himself as foam flew from the corners of his mouth behind him in a jet stream as the rabies propelled him through and toward even more carnage.

That first Santa, a guy named Stuart, had gravitated toward Rudy. The two had become good friends, and it was Stuart and his wife Lydia, who had stuck by Rudy after he was bitten in the forest during the equinox by a rabid werewolf. It was Lydia who had first founded the research and development department of the North Pole, and it was Lydia who had created the very first inhibitor collar. That had allowed Rudy to maintain his sanity and keep the virus at bay.

It was Stuart who had lost an arm hunting down the werewolf that had infected Rudy. Fortunately, a quick thinking yeti who witnessed the attack had ripped off Stuart's arm before the infection spread, and had caved in the wolf's head with a rock. Cauterizing the human stump with a burning log, the yeti had dragged his body near the Base and roared for attention before lumbering off into the trees. The medics had then been able to finish the job the yeti had started by saving Stuart's life.

Rabies works differently in Elves than it does in humans, and conventional medicine did not work as the virus took its hold over Rudy. Stuart and Lydia toiled for hours until finally, the first collar was made, and with a sense of fear and desperation, Rudy had agreed for Lydia to place it around his neck. It was either that or the machete that Stuart was holding. A choice of through or around the neck. Shaking with fever and perspiration, Rudy agreed to the collar.

It worked! Somehow the collar jammed the effects of the virus, unfortunately not destroying it. It stopped it from spreading, in fact, making it recede somewhere within the Elf's neural pathways. Rudy had immediately felt calmer, and slowly but surely Lydia had trusted her own invention enough to release the shackles that Rudy had allowed himself to be bound by.

He had never told them, but nothing made by man would have been strong enough to restrain an Elf. Humans would never have trusted them if they realized just how insanely strong Elves were, and just how easily they could have taken over Earth if they had chosen to. It had never been and would never be part of the Elven agenda.

Those aliens though…

In any case the collar had worked, and over time Rudy had worked with many Agents at the North Pole. With sadness, he had watched as time and accidents had taken friends from him, including Stuart and Lydia who after ten years at the North Pole had both succumbed to an entanglement with a wood chipper. He didn't want to think about that right now, he had a job to do. For all his friends back at the Base, and Nick and Carol who he had taken a liking to, despite not knowing them very well.

As Rudy made his way up the hill, he could see the big Santa more clearly, and what he saw stunned him. Covered in burnt and ripped red robes, the zombie glared down at him through its milky white eye and Rudy could make out a camera embedded into an orbital socket, zooming and twirling as the operator tried to get a bead on the rapidly moving Elf. All of a sudden, Rudy noticed the zombie sit still and punch downward. He heard a sound he didn't like. Then the mist cleared, confirming his worst fears. There, standing tall, yet torn to pieces was his friend Dasher with the big zombie sitting astride him.

"Oh dear boy, say it ain't so," he said. His reindeer friend did not respond, its dead eyes staring straight ahead as the Santa zombie booted the reindeer corpse in the ribs, and it rose from the ground slowly, propelling itself and its zombie cargo toward the Base.

With a battlecry, Rudy sprung into the air to try to catch onto any part of the reindeer he could. He needed to take that thing down, and for a brief moment his fevered mind thought he could make the jump, instead his outstretched fingers briefly touched the very edge of the matted, bloody fur of Dasher before falling to the earth as the reindeer flew on. And the zombie hordes followed, as they were commanded by a greater force than Rudy's living body.

He lay there, panting in the snow, his brain trying to process what had just happened, the rabies affecting his ability to think rationally. He had enough awareness remaining to know he had to get back to Base. He also knew that he had to get that thing back around his neck. The woman might have one, he couldn't remember her name. He got to his feet, wincing with the pain, which then kicked in the natural response of the rabies to overpower and dampen any other feeling. He howled again into the night and started moving rapidly back to Base.

A Christmas Carol

A nd now dear reader, the story comes full circle and we pick back up where we started. Carol heard Nick asking how she was going. She honestly didn't know herself. The minigun seemed utterly broken, and despite their best efforts, neither she nor the Elves could get it going again. She waved them away from it, telling them to pick up whatever ammunition they could get their hands on. It was disappointing. The damn thing could fire so fast it would mincemeat anything that moved. They wouldn't even have to worry about headshots, but unfortunately it wasn't going to be something they could take advantage of today.

She had shooed them away and could hear Nick's shotgun working furiously as he slammed round after round into it, swearing as he did so. She didn't like the fact that he was pumping so many rounds through without hearing protection. She was pretty sure he'd be going deaf, but she had an idea, and it would involve him giving her time to work uninterrupted. He was actually dipping the barrel of the shotgun into the snow, trying to cool it down, but they both knew that it was making the barrel brittle, and eventually there would be a round that broke it. She fiddled with some of the electronics on a project in front of her and looked down. She was pretty sure she was done.

Carol looked up from the workbench at Nick and said, "I think I'm finished." She held up one of the drones that they used to monitor the airspace of the North Pole. She had fashioned a launcher underneath it. It was spring loaded and she showed him the tranq dart it would fire. "So, the dart contains enough tranquilizer to knock one of these things down but not take it out," she said. "I'm simply not sure how their physiology works. I don't believe they can be poisoned as they are already dead."

Nick looked on as Carol packed the dart into the launcher module and they left the workshop, avoiding the straggling zombies there. There was not a lot of time left before the sleigh had to leave, and at this rate the place might be overrun soon. The attack seemed too coordinated to be a simple zombie attack. As far as Carol was concerned, she had seen enough zombie movies in her time to know that these things tended to not move with such focus, unless they were controlled by a force greater than themselves.

Radio chatter from the different Elf Teams indicated a larger zombie at the back of the battle that the other zombies seemed to respond to. Recent reports had it that all zombies were converging on the one location where the larger figure had been seen and were now moving en masse to the Toy Shop.

Carol got out the controller for the drone and threw the thing up into the air. Its tiny engine started, and the wings buzzed like an angry bumblebee. It hovered briefly, then she propelled it forward and up into the air. "This is our last chance," she said. "Has anyone heard from Rudy?" She fumbled quickly in her satchel and felt reassured. She had found notes from a previous female Agent that filled her knowledge in greater detail regarding Rudy and the collar program. She felt the hard outline of a collar in her bag and hoped that the Elf was okay and that she would be able to help him out should he need it.

The drone continued flying, sending back video footage of what was on the ground. She shuddered as she realized that the masses were actually a zombie horde, and that there were thousands of them. She watched as they shambled forward and the drone pulled back on the camera to reveal they were headed directly for the Base. The screen went dark and the drone flipped over and stopped there as it struck something. She quickly righted its flight path and zipped back a bit, moving alongside the thing it had struck. The drone's camera showed a bloodsoaked shaggy pelt.

Carol pulled back on the controller and the drone flew ahead and pivoted, its camera panning upward. Right there in front of her was the big Santa she had heard the reports about. Sitting on the back of one of her friends.

"You motherfucker," she snarled through gritted teeth. Nick saw the footage on her controller and glanced at her. "It's just you and me babe, no one else gets hurt tonight." He pushed a button on his wrist controller that set off yet another siren throughout the Toy Base; the general retreat siren. All the Elves, reindeer and other (redacted) knew what that meant; immediate retreat into the Toy Base, sealing doors, and initiating emergency lockdown protocols. Christmas this year was fucked and this alarm meant that unless something miraculous happened, Nick and Carol were also doomed.

The Elves were well trained, as were the reindeer, and all made their way inside as the huge hanger doors made of impenetrable concrete and steel closed with an ominous thud.

Nick put his arm around his wife's shoulder briefly and kissed her on the cheek. "Alright love, we've done our best. Let's get ready to kick some zombie ass. I just want you to know I loved you from the very first moment I laid eyes on you, and if today is the day it's time to go, there's no one I'd rather go with. Just you and me like it's always been."

Tears filled Carol's eyes, and she let go of one of the control sticks to caress her husband's cheek. She kissed him quickly, and turned her attention back to the monitor showing the drone footage.

"I only get one shot at this Nick, I don't even know what it will do, but I can try to shoot that dart at Dasher, and hopefully it will knock that fucker off his back. It'll slow him down, but I don't know what else to do." She bit her bottom lip as she concentrated; something she did unconsciously that Nick found as sexy as hell, and opened a switch on the controller. "Here goes nothing."

She pushed a button, and the footage showed the drone pushed backwards as a dart was fired. The footage was not good enough to see the flight, however the dead reindeer grunted as something smacked into it, and its flight path faltered. The zombie on its back did not react. It sat stupidly like a mannequin as the tranq serum kicked in and Dasher's corpse tipped over on its side and fell to Earth like a fur meteorite. Small victories. Carol smiled at Nick and they got ready to advance to where the enemy had fallen. The chances of getting through were slim; there were still thousands of zombies all under the control of the one main big guy, though with him falling to earth it might help a bit. As they walked, Carol kept the drone pointed down at the mass and out of the corner of the screen she saw a figure moving with inhuman speed through all the dead bodies. She activated the zoom on the camera and smiled. Nick looked at her questioningly, and Carol looked up. She showed Nick the controller, and he squinted at the screen, not able to figure out what he was looking at. She zoomed in some more, he still shook his head. "It's Rudy," she said. "He's alive."

There might still be a chance to turn this whole shit show around.

Rudy's Heroic Bloodbath

O n a small hill overlooking the zombie masses, Rudy could see ahead to the big building down below. Craning his neck up, he could see that big bastard on top of Dasher, when all of a sudden they both fell out of the sky. He couldn't figure out why that happened, and personally he didn't care. The main thing was it had stopped all the others from moving for the briefest of moments, which might give him a chance that he needed to get ahead of them.

Moving toward a thinning patch of the herd, Rudy hacked and slashed his way through masses of Santas, hearing the gurgling laughter as he did. Gore flew all over the place, coating his arms and clothing. The stuff coming out of these creatures was disgusting, not like the hot red blood of a living creature; it was cold and sticky as though it had congealed within their veins after they had died. Reanimation had not done a lot for them, either their looks or their intellect, and it kind of made Rudy glad to have rabies. He glanced behind him and saw the carnage left behind. It looked as though someone had laid down a zombie carpet for him to walk on. Up ahead was the Toy Shop, and he thought he could make out Nick and Carol (that was her name!) near the entrance to the hangar.

Why the heck were they by themselves? He wondered. The sight of Carol calmed him down a little. It was a curious feeling being able to think through the blood. Rage normally consumed him when the collar was off. He almost felt superhuman, that he could do anything. He continued to make his way through the waves of department store Santa zombies. He needed to get a move on.

Holly Jolly Massacre

Nick saw the horde stop as the big Santa and Dasher fell from the sky. The sickening sound of breaking bones was audible even from this distance, and yet he had a bad feeling that it was only the body of his friend cushioning the big Santa that he could hear, and sure enough the bastard slowly rose, and Nick felt as though it was staring directly at him and Carol. Then, as one, the creepy laughter started again. Even though he knew where it was coming from, it unnerved him.

In the back of his mind he wondered if sometimes the voice chips they put into some of the toys made the same sound. He made a mental note to make sure to play test some of these before next year's delivery.

That is of course if they even managed to get this year's delivery out. If the Toy Shop was fully locked up, it meant the sleigh could not get out even though hopefully the people inside would be safe. He'd already lost too many friends today, yet even so he felt bad about the delivery not taking place. They had a window now of about forty minutes before take off and the zombies were getting closer.

He heard Carol lift something next to him, and he looked to see what it was. She was holding a shoulder mounted rocket launcher, looking down the targeting reticule at the zombie masses.

"I'll probably only get the chance to get one shot off safely, but it might help Rudy just a little bit," she said. And fired. Flame shot out of the end of the launcher and the rocket flew straight and true into the horde closest to them. The shockwave from the detonation nearly knocked them off their feet and the zombies flew everywhere like pins in a bowling alley.

"Strike!" Carol yelled, and despite how messed up everything was, Nick laughed. Carol threw down the rocket launcher and picked up two fighting axes. "Where the hell are you getting all this shit from?" Nick asked in amazement. She always had a knack of finding things, but this was something next level.

"I'm always prepared love, but I think this time it really doesn't matter. We can't stop this many."

Carol paused for a moment considering something and turned to Nick with a thoughtful look on her face as she put down the axes and took her laptop out of the case on the ground. "Honey? Did you notice when we shot the thing that used to be Dasher down with the big guy on his back, everyone seemed to stop?"

Nick scratched his beard. "I haven't really given it much thought. I was concentrating too much on the massive fucking zombie army that it was on its way to tear us apart." He chuckled, "But now that you mention it, yes. They did seem to stop. He is a big bastard isn't he?"

"It's not so much his size, it's how he uses it," she joked. "But no, seriously, they did stop when he fell and started to move again once he got back up. I think there's a slight possibility that these fuckers are being controlled by something outside this facility, and it's all being channelled through the big one. Keep an eye out for me. I'm going to scan the immediate area for frequencies that are unknown to our systems."

Carol plugged something into the computer, a small satellite looking dish about the size of a dinner plate. It started rotating on its stand, and he could see information appearing on the laptop screen. There was a blip on the radar. He pointed and said "Is that it?" She nodded. "Yes, I think so. That is coming from an external source. In fact, I can actually pinpoint it."

She quickly triangulated the position, her fingers blazing across the keys like lightning with the speed at which she typed. After a moment, she pointed skyward and said that's where it is. Nick said, "What's that? What are you talking about?"

"There's a transmission coming in from a satellite near the Edge of the World. You know how they put those beacons up there to stop stuff from flying into nothing? Well, from what I can figure, there's one tethered there; a small communication satellite no bigger than a car and it's beaming down into that mass." She pointed at the zombies.

"I'm only considering this because that fucker got airborne, that he may be the receiver of whatever commands have been given, which means there's a third-party who is not here that is controlling these Santa zombies, so I would surmise that if

114

I can hack that signal then maybe I can figure out who is doing this to us. Keep an eye out love."

The laptop was making a gentle pinging sound. It sounded like the sonar of a submarine in a movie. "There's all sorts of encryption on the signal," she said. Nick shrugged, "You know I don't know anything about that sort of thing, that was always your jam. I'm more of a run and gun kinda guy."

The horde was closer now, and Nick pulled out his pistol, headshotting those who got too close. Occasionally, he'd miss or not destroy the brain, and they kept moving closer and closer. In the background, body parts were being thrown up in the air as though a hay plow was going through the Undead.

The big Santa had gotten up, as had Dasher's corpse, though its neck was weirdly bent at an angle.

Carol's fingers danced over the keyboard as she struggled to break the transmission going through to the mind of the lead Santa zombie. She was also getting an IP address that she was pretty sure she could route back to its origin. The numbers crystallized, and formed a singular address that made sense, she made a note of them; she would need them for later. *Bye for now.* She smashed down the keyboard and high up in the sky overhead they heard an explosion and pieces of satellite hurtled to the ground below in a metal rain. Other chunks fell over the Edge of the World and into the abyss. No doubt they would later be discovered by the aliens. She'd have to ask Mike the Alien about that later.

The Day the Laughter Died.

T he big Santa shattered violently to a halt. The gurgling laughter was replaced with a solemn "No, no, no," which sputtered out and died. But the big guy kept on coming, and the herd behind him was not so far back that they couldn't see the expressions on the dead faces as they made their way shambling through the snow. It looked as though there were not that many left now. Their numbers had thinned considerably.

Carol looked in the background and could see a whirling dervish of body parts being thrown into the air like a crazy, airborne meat grinder. Zombie Santas were being spewed haphazardly throughout the atmosphere as their body parts rained down to the snow below, freezing in place. *Someone's gotta clean that up,* she thought to herself.

A green speck was in the center of all the action, with snow and blood flowing all around it. It was Rudy. She smiled to herself and pointed him out to Nick. Nick paused briefly, then kept pumping shots through the shotgun. Not many rounds left. They hadn't really thought this out well, ordering everyone else back inside without restocking. It was going to be close. Nick pointed at his watch. He had fifteen minutes before that sleigh had to get airborne regardless of what happened, and if the herd was still out here, that just wasn't gonna happen. Christmas was going to be wrecked for everyone. Including all the counter surveillance devices that were hidden underneath the damn thing. If those didn't get up, they would set The Agency back at least a year of new technology hovering above the planet. At least on this side of the earth. He didn't know how they monitored the other side. He'd heard that they dug a hole all the way through, and there was a secret lift, but he didn't have the clearance and quite frankly at the moment he didn't care.

In the back of his mind, a soundtrack played as he watched the carnage play out in front of him, 'Ride of the Valkyries.' That would be adequate for the amount of blood and guts that was spewing all over in the back of the herd and making its way forward.

It looked as though there were other things in the swirling snow with Rudy. It briefly cleared and he could see the source of the carnage and he knew there was too much gore for just one creature, despite how powerful it may be. Oh. My. God. It was the yetis.

There had been reports for the longest time that these things were out here, and he would've sworn he had seen at least one. The Elves tried to cover it up though, saying it was just a big shaggy homeless man. What did they say his name was? Floyd? Yep, that was it. It was said that Floyd lived out here somewhere but they could never get a bead on his actual location. Yetis, who would've thought it? Nick had thought they had all but vanished ever since the first Santa had reported one.

The yeti's made their way through the zombie pack with ease, slicing and dicing and ripping things apart with huge arms. Rudy jumped up and over their backs, using them as a platform for overhead attacks, his nimble Elven fingers swirling their way through brains, bone and sinew. The Herd had been decimated, and it was only a matter of time before they were all –

Dead of Christmas

Nick heard a choking sound right next to him. Why the hell hadn't he been paying attention? The huge Santa zombie lifted Carol up into the air with one arm, electronics sputtering out of its head and its broken eye. She lifted both of her hands up to try to pry its one powerful claw away from her throat and kicked frantically, her legs smashing against the monster in her red outfit. The woman he loved was about to die unless he did something fast. And he had nothing.

Looking at the shotgun which was empty, and no more rounds left in the pouch around his waist, he did the one thing he could and swung the weapon by the barrel as hard as he could, shattering the hip of the Santa, which was almost as high as his head. This thing was massive. None of the video footage did it any justice; it was an abomination. And then it dawned on him, it wasn't an abomination; it was in fact, a reanimated yeti.

The Santa fell on its side, but didn't release its grip on Carol. It dragged itself up onto its knees and still held her above its head. Her face was going scarlet and Nick, try as he might, couldn't release the grip this thing had on his wife's neck. He got too close and it swung out, knocking him into the ground, meters away, too far away to be of any help. His wife was looking at him, and even in the struggle, he could see her love.

Here's Rudy

The green blob that has been in the background the entire time during the battle flew overhead, its face streaked with blood. Its uniform was torn to shreds by thousands of grasping, hungry hands. Time seemed to slow, and Nick could see Rudy's face clearly. His handsome features were still visible under the gore and he would've sworn he could see the Elf wink at him as he flew overhead. Rudy reached into one of the remaining pockets on his jacket, and as he flew through the air, somersaulted forward so that his feet were driving downward. Something shiny was in his hand, and he booted Carol in the chest as he missed the zombie's head. The force knocked her loose and she flew backwards, striking the ground hard, but looking back the entire time. Rudy had gripped the zombie by its neck and was still holding the shiny thing in his hand. She knew what it was and looked the Elf in the eye.

Rudy pushed the button on the silver thing, which was Rudolph's thermal detonator and it made a high-pitched whine. There were four seconds left on the fuse, and she calculated that both she and Nick were clear of its blast. Rudy looked at her and then his calm, lovely voice spoke to her. It was audible above the blizzard and the roars of the big Santa, "This is for you my dear, and of course for Lydia. Sweet Lydia."

Rudy jammed the thermal detonator into the gnashing teeth of the Santa zombie, and with both arms, closed its jaws tight. The explosive force of the detonator ripped both bodies to shreds, sending meat flying all over the place. Hot pieces of flesh fell onto the snow, melting it instantly, creating a cacophony of hissing noises as the snow parted. Rivulets of blood made their way down this nightmare incline toward Carol with meat and gristle stuck in them but she didn't notice a thing. All she was aware of was her beloved Nick running to her, and of the sacrifice that Rudy had made. She didn't see the Elves running out of the Toy Shop, she didn't notice Mike the Alien looking down at her near her shoes as he crouched. She didn't see what he did. All she saw was Nick who cradled her in his arms and told her that everything was going to be okay. That was the only thing she needed right now.

Lift Off

Nick's voice broke through all of the white noise. "The sleigh is ready babe, I've gotta go," he said. She was puzzled, "Go where?" He pointed backwards to where the sleigh was now being dragged out to the airfield. "We've got about three minutes. Are you okay?"

She nodded. She didn't feel any injuries though she knew that she probably wouldn't be able to speak tomorrow once her throat had swollen. One of the medics was already treating her. Nick looked at the Elf who gave him the thumbs up. It was going to be okay. "Well little lady, I have an idea. It's against protocol, but I think we can make an exception. What would you say about going on a road trip?"

Back at the sleigh they could see the Elves already laying an extra blanket on the passenger seat. Carol smiled and kissed him on the cheek. "There's nothing I'd like more," she croaked. He gently lifted her up like he had the first time he carried her across a threshold in that house, at that place that was part of a redacted file at Agency Headquarters. Carefully, he took her up the ramp, and placed her in the sleigh, getting behind the reigns himself. The eleven reindeer... Yes, he

123

reminded himself. There were only eleven now. Poor Dasher. Blitzen looked back from the head of the pack. "Are you ready boss?"

"Yes my friend, let's rock. And Blitzen?"

"Yes Boss?"

"Thank you."

He put his arm around his wife, and Carol snuggled into the crook of his shoulder. The reindeer carefully made their way forward being mindful of Carol. Normally the guys would race forward on Christmas Eve, giving him whiplash in the process, but tonight the sleigh made its way into the night sky with an ease and grace that belied its bulk. Nick and Carol flew toward the Edge of the World and circled back toward the lights of foreign countries beckoning them. The thing that was controlling those damn zombies were still out there. They both knew it, and that would have to be dealt with. What they weren't sure of was how much of the world was actually left, and that was a problem for another time. For now, this was Christmas Eve and he was going to make sure that he took his wife under every sprig of mistletoe he possibly could.

Epilogue

D eep under the Toy Shop there's a lab that no one talks about. That's because hardly anyone knows it exists. It's so heavily classified that there are only two human beings in the entire world that know about it. And they are not Nick and Carol. An array of blinking machines did their thing as lab technicians in white coats adjusted the very strands of life itself.

Mike the Alien stopped in front of two test tubes and looked at the read out that was coming out of the computer next to it. The alien gave a long blink and looked at his counterpart. They both looked at the test tubes. These were huge things filled with liquid, but in the middle, life was growing. In one, a tiny reindeer kicked and struggled its way through the muck, its fur growing rapidly. In the other, a little humanoid figure swam, almost seeming content. Mike the Alien knew that would be impossible. It would be at least five hours before Rudy had grown big enough to remember what had happened, even longer before Dasher would be able to return to the stables.

"Are you sure you want them to remember everything?" Jim the lab tech asked Mike the Alien. "Yes, I think it's important for both them and everyone else. I guess the main thing is to make sure they don't remember this part of the adventure," Mike the Alien said. Jim laughed. Of course. He made some notes and adjustments on the computer, then looked at Mike the Alien. "You know that we can fix him up," he pointed a long spindly finger at Rudy. "We can if you want to, that is we can get rid of the rabies."

Mike the Alien thought long and hard. He thought this might be an option, but then again, sometimes it was best to leave things the way they were. He looked at Jim and said, "No. Leave the rabies in. I think he likes it." He turned and walked up the long corridor towards the light leading outside and vanished.

END?

COMING TO YOUR EYEBALLS IN 2024, THE SEQUEL TO THE DEAD OF CHRISTMAS: THE DEAD OF EGYPT

The Dead of Egypt

"**M**otherfucker!" Mike the Alien looked around. Sand blew into his huge black eyes and he wiped a gray hand across his face. The shit was everywhere. He fumbled around in his jeans pockets for a pair of sunglasses. Nothing. He looked down in the pocket of his Hawaiian shirt. Yup, there looking back up at him were his black glasses, specially made for him by none other than the Elves at the North Pole.

He whipped them around his eyes, wrapping them at the back of his head. Sometimes he wished he had a nose. *Oh well*, he thought *you can't always have what you wish for*. Speaking of wishing for anything, he really thought that when he teleported at the end of the last book, he would've been back at the North Pole, but no, here he was somewhere hot and sandy, and getting grit in his eyes, at least at the North Pole when it snowed it turned to water pretty quickly, unless you were trapped out there drunk. That had happened more than once, something he was able to laugh off now, though every now and then the Elves would still post pictures of him with no pants on.

He never knew what the hang up was with clothing. His people did not wear anything, they really didn't need it. It

127

was humans and their desire to cover up their skin all the time. He tried to do the right thing, and cover up as best he could, though, to be honest, it wasn't as though he had any visible genitalia.

The last thing he remembered was being back at the North Pole, looking at some dead friends re-growing in a tank filled with liquid even he had trouble identifying. He had left the laboratory, and had teleported the short distance back to where he had last been seen. Except now he was nowhere near that fucking place. Instead of being in the cold of the North Pole, wherever the hell this place was, was batshit hot. And windy. And worst of all, sandy as all get out. Maybe there was a reason why humans like to wear clothes, he thought to himself as he scratched through his pants where his groin would have been if he had one.

TURN THE PAGE TO FIND OUT JUST WHAT THE HELL IS GOING ON IN EMERALD CITY!

TIN MAN

Book One in the Emerald City Novel series
by **TORY FAVRO.**

You always thought you knew this **STORY**
Now it is time to see just how **WRONG** you were.
The place…..

EMERALD CITY

The most corrupt city in the **UNITED STATES OF AMERICA,** controlled by **GREEDY CORPORATIONS** and the **GANG**. Everything in Emerald City is for sale. For a **PRICE**.

UNTIL NOW.

When Gang Enforcer **THE TIN MAN**, Tin Manning, discovers child pit fighter **DOROTHY** in a dumpster left for **DEAD**, it sets about a chain of events that will change both their lives forever. A tale of **BLOODY REVENGE** and **MAYHEM** sets the city afire and their lives will never again be the same.

BULLETS. BLOOD. MAYHEM and FAMILY

Welcome to the City. Emerald City. Filled with characters you might think you know, but with a fresh new spin. Spanning seven action packed novels, each book can be read separately or as part of an ongoing saga. Click your heels if you can, because there's no place like home in the world quite like Emerald. Oh yes we are off to see the **WIZARD, MOTHERF**KER!**

Printed in Great Britain
by Amazon

34644501R00076